the UNMAKING

CAROL BIRCH

AVAILABLE
PRESS

BALLANTINE BOOKS
NEW YORK

An Available Press Book
Published by Ballantine Books

Copyright © 1992 by Carol Birch

All rights reserved under International and Pan-American Copyright
Conventions. Published in the United States by Ballantine Books, a
division of Random House, Inc., New York, and simultaneously
in Canada by Random House of Canada Limited, Toronto.

Library of Congress Catalog Card Number: 92-90067
ISBN: 0-345-37804-0

Cover design by Barbara Leff
Cover painting: *The Lovers in the Country,
Sentiments of Youth, Paris* (detail) by Gustave Courbet.
Courtesy of the Musée du Petit Palais, Paris.

Manufactured in the United States of America
First Edition: November 1992
10 9 8 7 6 5 4 3 2 1

For Mic Cheetham

❖ THE UNMAKING ❖

t Caddenhope, Rennock lived with a daughter and a son. The old man had been dying for so long now that the event was no longer anticipated, and he lived in his bed by the window, where he could look out and see the fields and the distant forest where he'd never go again.

This left his children with a great deal of freedom: Belle, his daughter, had taken for her lover a young man so unsuitable that she was forced to flit out and meet him in secret, sometimes in the middle of the night. This was not so great a hardship, as she particularly liked the dead of night and had never been able to sleep then, even before the deception began. She even liked the fear. She liked the hating of the waiting for the house to be still enough, watching the candle burn away till it stood diminished, hunch-necked, the flame quivering a little from time to time as if an irregular pulse beat inside it. She couldn't bear it. She liked the wriggling and turning on the bed, fully clothed and ready to go, sighing and relishing the danger as she beat her heels or placed her thin white hand carelessly over the place she thought of as her heart.

IT felt a little sick there. She jumped up and stood holding the bed curtain, looking startled. She didn't have to go out, she could undress and crawl between the sheets and go to sleep, but her room was remote already, blue and ghostly, familiar things gone strange. A cage hung in the window, its occupant asleep on the perch under a swiftly thrown cloth. 'Sh!' she told it needlessly, pulling her mantle round her and drawing the hood down over her face.

Half way down the stairs she started to laugh and had to bite on her fingers to quell it. Sin was the stuff of her life, the terror of it was always with her. Sin was what made her do these terrible things, made her want to bite John Heron's neck. The dirt on his hands was so deep it would never come out, she thought. Like Sin. More than a year and she didn't care and couldn't stop and wouldn't. She loved Sin. It was unspeakable. She couldn't stop laughing.

The dogs knew but never told. One lifted its head and yawned, one tiredly beat its rope-like tail twice. She went out through the kitchen door and ran like a mouse on her soft shoes across the cobbles of the yard, out onto the cinder path that led to the road. It was May, mild enough, and the moon was full. Her teeth chattered, but not with cold. She walked quickly, with purpose, between dark stands of beech, then open scrub where she struck out for higher ground, walking on the wide verges. Anyone seeing her would have thought she must be silly in the head to walk so assuredly without a light, so late, so close to where the forest began. But she wasn't afraid of the dark, only of Hell. She wouldn't think about it. A heavy night bird flew across the sky, and she stumbled and dipped both feet in a shallow stream that crossed her path. The icy water, cruel as knives, brought tears to her eyes and caught at her breath, and she stood in the damp grass looking down at her feet, for a moment really unsure if she was asleep or awake; the two were so similar lately.

She was in the Sallow Meadow where the old barn stood; and there, when she looked back, was all that she knew, the long valley where the ploughs got a hold near the shores of the forest, the great shaggy god that filled the land from one sea to another. The forest climbed mountains and plunged deep into valleys, covered everything just as moss covered the stones in the rankest, dampest parts of itself. It was like fur on the back of a beast, clearing for paws and nose and belly and rump, the thinnings where bony cattle grazed and black-faced sheep with red badges swung their long tails in the broom, and buildings clustered together for safety, spires and halls and barns and byres and the hovels of the poor.

She did not go to the barn immediately, though she thought she could make out, even from here, the pale glow of a lantern through the crack at the side of the door. That was dangerous. Like Sin, danger ran in her blood, screwing her up to a bright pitch of excitement.

What could she do?

When she was fourteen she'd lain on her bed and squirmed, thinking of how he stood when he rested in the field, his neck fragile like the stem of a flower; and how he stood when he knew he was watched, manly, shoulders squared and one leg thrust sideways. She loved his big innocence and his lopsided mouth with the broken tooth. He was eighteen, soft-eyed, full of smiles, and the skin at the corners of his eyes was cracked like leather, his hands old. She'd watched him working with mud on his hose, fingers sticking out of his mittens, sweating like his oxen, coarse brown hair clinging to his head as theirs did to their massive flanks. How the great patient beasts stood, Taurus on earth, champing and snorting and blinking their sad brown eyes as he talked to them, tenderly kneading their steaming necks when he took off their harness. The muscles twitched, de-lighted, exhausted.

And one day she'd spoken.

She had sinned now, she supposed, at least a thousand times. What else could she possibly do? He wore a grey coat, and ate oatcakes with a lump of cheese for his dinner. His voice drawled with that accent they all had, stretching the vowels.

His face was brown; they were all brown.

He smelt different; they all did—

He was utterly forbidden.

Towards dawn the house grew restless.

Hugh Rennock woke up in the darkness and heard the crowing of a cock and the coughing of his father, constant and distant like the croaking of an amorous toad. He hoped he wasn't there when the old man retched himself out of this world and into the next on a quick gush of blood from the mouth. That's how it would be. Blood in the chase Hugh found thrilling, bright and sticky on a brown flank, but the blood of his father he feared. He thought it would be different from the good red blood of the young, thicker, darker, perhaps rusty. Perhaps he would faint at it, like a girl.

He was parched. His beard smelt of stale red wine. He drew the curtain and drank water thirstily from a jug that stood on the floor beside the bed, then got up, yawning mightily, shivering naked in the night air and pulling the bed-cover about himself, wishing he were a better sleeper. Thank God the old man had been moved downstairs. His own throat, acrid with excess, tightened at the carking tone that hacked on and on, thick with blood and mucus. When he did die, Hugh would be rich. He'd need a steward.

He hawked and spat into his chamber pot, then pissed after the spot of phlegm, groaning with relief. He was hunting today. At the window he looked vainly for dawn, sniffing the air and guessing the weather. Fine. The yard was bright, unearthly. His thoughts ran on through the woods with the long hounds and the little beaters, and he smiled, dreaming of hot horseflesh and fresh young leaves, and all the lovely stirring din of it. Harlock would ride at the head hallooing with the best, urging on his men, his broad red face taut. Harlock liked him. Harlock was a noisy, bluffish old soul, growing ridiculous—

A cloaked and hooded figure stood where the cinder path came into the yard. Hugh feared nothing as much as the supernatural. His teeth clicked and the palms of his hands sweated. 'Sweet Jesus, sweet Jesus, sweet Jesus,' he breathed and suddenly the yard seemed ghastly. The figure flitted like a great black moth to the kitchen door, where a hand with thin, pointed fingers appeared and lifted the latch.

It was Belle.

His scalp still crawled. His anger was huge, for he'd been badly frightened. It was she, he knew the hand. What was she doing, creeping about in the middle of the night outside? Putting fear in him? Was she mad?

He turned to the door, all hot and confused, thinking he would run out on the landing and grab her wrist and ask her what in Hell's name she thought she was doing, but something stopped him and instead he sat down upon the bed and licked his dry lips slowly, an expression of sad bewilderment on his ruddy face.

Once they'd been very close but he did not know her any more. She was getting too grand. Lately she snapped and sulked and shrugged away from him, and he found himself wanting to hit her. Better to watch for a while, he thought, just watch. If it was some secret, she'd never tell him.

Why wasn't she afraid? She *ought* to be afraid. Then he remembered how she had said, coming into his room when his nightmares roused him—even then, the things had plagued him—Hugh, it's only the dark. Morning soon. Only the dark. Looking about, he wondered why he felt so strange. That she should appear in a situation so unnatural seemed horrible to him, as if his horse had got up on tip-toes and walked like a man. It was not in the order of things; it threatened chaos.

She stood in her room laughing into her hands, leaning a little forward from the hips as if telling someone something funny.

Dawn was rising. A few fingers of pale light appeared on the wall, slanting like God's blessing towards the small green parrot in the cage, whose cover had been thrown so roughly and slipped so much during the night, that he was more than half uncovered. He began to mutter sleepily, shifting a little on the perch and ruffling his neck feathers slightly.

'Sh!' she hissed, finger on lips. 'Sh!'

She heard the coughing of her father. A board creaked somewhere. Morning was too close. She undressed and lay down with the covers pulled up to her chin, though it would not be for long. If anyone should come she could say: I have been here all night. She began to cry as her blood slowed down. She did not believe, even now, what she had done. It could not go on. She knew it could not go on. Even as it continued it was impossible, and she hated impossibility. Every time, it was as if she walked on the lip of a great rock with nothing below but gaping air, as if her foot slipped and she began to fall, as if she caught, just in time, the overhanging branch of a friendly tree. And there she hung.

he forest was mazy, impenetrable in places. It could madden and deceive and amaze all at once. Hugh loved it, particularly on a day such as this, when the small new leaves were casting a dappled shade and drift upon drift of wild green tracery rose to the far blue of the sky. The hunt dispersed some of the mystery: everything rang to the music of horn and voice and the terrible, shrill, delightful crying of the hounds. It was thrilling and wild and nothing compared to it. If somewhere the forest had a heart, deep and dark and beyond imagining, it stirred, drawing its trembling creatures closer, as dogs draw closer to the heat of the fire when draughts creep under the door.

They took several boar. One fine sow, her litter about her, blundered into one of the dog stations and went mad, downing the bravest lymer with a single stroke. The poor bitch whimpered as she died, long mouth laughing gamely while the boy whetted his knife, and the sow broke through, running amongst the thickets with the thin striped bodies of her offspring dashing squealing this way and that. Some the dogs killed, four were taken to be reared, and a spear finished off their mother.

Up ahead was a massive bristling fiend of a thing with horrible tusks, swift and subtle and wily as the devil, moving through the matted undergrowth as if it were water and he a fish. They clamoured after him like clumsy swimmers. Nearing noon he was still ahead, leading them higher and higher along a craggy ridge, till they knew they must have him soon as they ringed and ringed him in, on their left a gully with sudden edges and illusory tracks, where boulders shifted at a touch, rocking over empty air. He vanished too suddenly. The dogs screamed with frustration and the horsemen pulled on the bits, wary. There was much beating of the bushes. Someone told a story about a mad goat that came down from a hill one day and bit a woman so that she died, and when they came to kill it, it called upon the devil with a human voice. And someone mentioned Bayardine.

Lord Harlock ordered a halt. Hugh Rennock was a great favourite with him and they took a drink together on a pleasant bluff overlooking Herndale, where the river bent like a great bow through little fields and gentle hills, before the trees once more concealed it. Herndale had come to Harlock through his wife. It was beautiful, Hugh thought, but he could never see it without thinking of the grimness of its history. He well remembered the burning, though he'd seen nothing and heard much. She'd been a local woman, her brood more or less grown. The poor stared and starved, and their children cried. Hers thrived. Food from the devil, they said. He'd lain awake in the dark, imagining all the things they'd done to the witch's daughter, seventeen years old. He was thirteen then, and Belle was a small child.

He cleared his throat.

Harlock lounged, lost in thought as he grimaced in the glare of the sun, his big red face sweating. 'The lovely spoiled place,' he said heavily. He made everything sound like foolery.

'What?' said Hugh.

'That is what my wife calls that place,' Harlock said expansively. 'It was hers. She never went there since the burnings. Couldn't keep her away at one time.'

'I would like to speak to you about my sister, Isabel,' Hugh said.

'Belle,' said Harlock distantly, fingering some crimson silk at his throat. 'Yes. And is she well?'

'The marriage should be soon,' said Hugh, and gestured. 'She is . . . restless and troublesome and—' she fell into waking dreams, cried suddenly, snapped and fretted—even cursed—sat staring into the fire as if she saw there the world's doom, and now, now she crept into the house like a ghost returning to its bed at dawn.

All this he did not say. He went cold there in the kind spring air. The voices of the men in Harlock's colours rose and fell, the bridles jingled, and the sound of a cuckoo came into his left ear. Bewitched. Oh Lord, all this talk of evil.

'Your father is dying,' Harlock said. 'Little wonder she behaves strangely.'

Hugh frowned. His bones told him this was not the cause. 'She should be married,' he said bluntly.

Harlock nodded, scarcely concealing a sigh. This was tiresome. 'Well, well,' he said placatingly, 'soon enough. William will never be more ready.' And never any better, he added in thought. The boy was a gnat in his eye, but the time was not right. Labour came dear these days, damn the plague. 'We'll speak of it again,' he said vaguely. 'What are the fools talking about? Sim? Sim!'

Harlock's boy appeared, a smirk-faced little villain with a pushed-up nose and skinny legs. 'Sir?'

'What are they talking about?'

'They're saying the boar went through a secret door put there by Bayardine.' The boy told it with suppressed delight, as if it were a delicious understated joke.

Harlock laughed. He still had all his teeth and they were fine and strong and yellow like the back teeth of a ram's skull that's been lying out on the heath for a year. Then he spat, and his eyes were hard. 'Tell them I forbid superstition,' he said.

The boy bowed and went.

'That particular demon'—Harlock articulated it as if his fine teeth were coated in gum—'has no being.' He stood up, flexing his powerful body and thrusting out his padded chest. One hand, a big jade ring on the finger, stroked the thin grey hairs that curled very prettily at the back of his neck. 'And if he did,' he continued, walking towards his horse, 'he'd get what the others got—the fire.'

When? Hugh wanted to shout. The man was exasperating. The marriage. When? He followed and stood stroking the soft grey nose of his mare, watching as the older man beat his gloved hands together.

'Better still.' Harlock's thin lips made square corners and his voice was clipped and small. 'The gallows, slowly.' He looked about with an air of pique before concluding, 'Then hew him into morsels and send him about the kingdom.' Satisfied, he put his foot in the stirrup.

Someone brought news that the quarry had been scented at the far side of Ellwin Beck.

'Not Bayardine then,' said Harlock, landing heavily in the saddle. The tall black steed tottered, its nostrils flaring like its master's. Both looked a little mad, in the way that pups or wild birds do. A bugle sounded. The forest stirred.

'I must know more than this,' Hugh said shortly, mounting his horse.

Harlock reined back a little. Hugh's face was slightly hand-some, slightly coarse, with round brown eyes and a thick nose, a mouth much given to moving. It was sulky now, the thick lower lip pronounced. This was insolence, but Harlock was fond of the young man.

'Come to Ellwin,' he said kindly. 'My wife's birthday is next month. Bring your sister. She must renew her acquaintance with William. How long is it since they met?'

He spurred his horse and it mounted the bank clumsily.

'Years,' Hugh whispered gloomily to himself.

THE boar was at bay, his back in the brake, foam and the blood of the hounds he'd maimed streaking the great clashing tusks.

His head was low, with ears pressed flat, and the little red eyes turning their gleam from nowhere to nowhere. They always look at me, thought Hugh, and the look always chilled him in the heat of the day. Whispering arrows flew, some sticking amongst the bristles, some glancing off and falling to the ground. One hung down bent from below the eye. Hugh joined his voice to the madness in the air, raised fury, turned his blood savage, the smell of fear and blood churning his bowels. The boar was a monster, a raging, snarling, foul-mouthed monster with great dirty pig feet stamping thunder out of the ground.

It charged the line, felling a man and scattering more, running into the next relay, where it stumbled in a shaded drift of small white flowers. Harlock himself finished it off, striking home beautifully between the shoulders and thrusting hard till the beast was impaled to the cross of the spear, bellowing abominably and stiffening its limbs.

A great cheer arose. The boar's tail swished when he was down. His dumb eye moved, saying nothing. Then the dogs covered him and he was wrenched, nose separated from jaw, tail from croup, his little red eyes still saying nothing. Thin white teeth tore nape and heels and belly and breast, and the cheer went on, falling, to rise again with the blaring of the horns and the baying of the hounds.

They went triumphant through the forest to the station nearest the beck. The game was heaped near a bank of early violets, the tally taken. The unmaking was performed. A fire was lit. Harlock dealt with the boar, rolling back his sleeves and skilfully wielding the fine silver blades and the little silver fork. No more salt meat, thought Hugh, looking at the men standing round in jolly, raucous knots, blowing their noses into their hands. The smell of fresh blood reached his nostrils as his racing heart abated, and the cheer went round and round, and the heaps of shining flesh grew higher. Someone stuck the severed head on a stick and it was passed around, and they raised its lips to see its teeth,

and breathed the rankness of its snout. From the fire a delicious
aroma rose into the warm air: blooded bread, offal, the beast's
huge testicles—the feast for the hounds, who whined in antici-
pation, flapping moisture from the ends of their long tongues.

He smelt ale.

Like black flags, or rags of soot from a fire, the ravens and
crows came slowly flapping, gathering in the fragrant trees,
awaiting pacification.

HUGH rode home with the sound of the horns still ringing in
his ears. The clouds were fat and white in a flat blue sky. Bees
hovered in the gorse. From the top of a rise he saw Caddenhope
and spurred lightly down to it, growing leisurely as he neared
home, the patient grey neck of Serafina nodding before him.

Belle's face kept getting into his mind. The thought that she
might stray wounded him more than he understood, and made
him want to harm her and protect her from harm all at the same
time. She was always in his sight and he never thought of her,
and he'd kill her if she changed. She was not a fool. Where did
she go? What did she do when he was away? Why, surely, she
was with her father.

But she was bold sometimes, and she loved her own company. He remembered her as a child who had worshipped him,
and a sudden pang shot him through, as if a child were dying.

Tread carefully, he thought.

The fields lay about him. Cattle grazed with their puny
young. Slow, inexorable, the plough moved like time. At the
end of the furrow the oxen rested, dropping their heads, and the
boy pushed the yoke forward to let the cooling air soothe their
necks. Hugh bit his lip. The peaceful scene made him angry and
he kicked with his heels. Serafina surged forward, down to the
low rambling house.

He found her in the parlour where their father's bed had been made up. Rennock lay propped on pillows, his hollow, wrinkled face ghastly. The bed was crowded. Belle sat upon it, picking her nails over a chessboard that had been laid aside. Her face was carefully pale, long-featured, lacking brows. Her eyes seemed half asleep, so heavy were the lids, and her mouth was sulky. He had always been fascinated by her throat, which was long and lively and gave away her feelings in a way her eyes did not. He felt pride in such a sister, and felt in some obscure way that he had raised her, as if such a man as he was had nurtured a rare white flower from a seed.

She'd be content with William, vapid thing with his nose-bleeds. There was no harm there. She'd live well.

'Will you want supper?' she asked, glancing up. 'We weren't sure.' She wore a green girdle and her fair hair was stiffly braided on either side of her face. A small dog ranged about her on the bed-cover. A lean white cat rolled onto its belly and stretched. After the vigour of the chase, this somnolence made Hugh itch.

'Thank you,' he said, irritated. 'We had wonderful sport.'

She smiled thinly, suppressing a yawn.

'He knows nothing. The doctor knows nothing,' said Rennock towards the window, unaware that his son had come into the room.

Belle sighed and tapped the spotted hen's claw that protruded grimly from her father's sleeve. 'Twelve,' she said.

'Twelve?' echoed Hugh.

'Twelve times he's said that today.' She looked fully at him then and smiled. Hugh returned the smile. Ridiculous, he thought. His father turned his head, the pendulous flesh of his throat moving softly. Noticing Hugh, he was shy.

'Father,' Hugh said, nodding politely, appalled. He'd been terrified of this man, this bundle of old flesh that smelt as if it were dead already, that scratched at fleas feebly and needed its mouth wiped when it fed, grinning vacantly like some old fool begging for alms. His father begged time and smiles, someone to push a pawn about on a board and tell him how lucky he was to be in out of the rain. He'd not been out for a year. Hugh had to tell all, embellishing, the chase, the kill, the tally, the strength and cunning of the boar, and again, as he loved to hear, the favoured state of his son in Lord Harlock's company—as if that were any wonder. After all, thought Hugh, we are the second family hereabouts.

'Which brings me,' said Hugh, shifting his gaze to Belle and smiling like a father bestowing a gift upon a child, 'to the real news of the day. We are invited to Ellwin. There's to be a feast, a very grand affair I'm sure, for the birthday of the old man's wife. He particularly wishes you to be there, Belle.'

Rennock was overcome by a fit of coughing that gushed water from his eyes and nose, and a little blood from his mouth.

'For May?' she said guilelessly, leaning over to rub the old man's back and wipe his face. 'A feast?'

' "She must renew her acquaintance with William." That's what he said. He must be quite a young buck by now.' Hugh watched her closely while appearing not to.

Her mouth tightened as she straightened the cushions, settling the gasping head against them and waiting till the spasm had passed. 'I can't go,' she said, then, 'Father's too sick.' She looked away, out of the window.

Rennock had found his voice and protested with all his remaining strength that she would go or he'd know the reason why.

'A few hours,' Hugh said. 'Father will spare you, I am sure.'

'It's Harlock, you fool!' the old man wheezed. 'You can't insult them by not going!'

Belle looked at Hugh. He may die upon that night, they both thought. Hugh's lips made a quick, disclaiming movement. He may die upon that night or he may live another year. He might even live to see her wed.

'Harlock wishes it,' said Hugh importantly. 'He told me.'

Then real ill temper swelled her face like fever, and she bit her nails. Tears filled her eyes. 'I don't want to go,' she said.

Hugh was suddenly furious. Of course she wanted to go. *Once* she would have.

He turned and walked out, ordered some supper to be left in his room then went out to the mews, which soothed him with its shadowy light and smell of turf, the gentle susurration of feathers as a bird stirred upon a perch. The fierceness of Phoebe, his best hawk, raised his spirits. She sat with one foot tucked up, delving sometimes into the softness of her barred grey breast with a deadly beak, rousing occasionally and regarding him with cold indifference and a certain wild pride that never failed to stir his blood. Her round orange eye was bright and clear as honey. Hugh stiffened in remembrance of perfect kills.

Belle came in and stood beside him, playing with a yellow silk veil that she'd pulled down from her hair. She did not speak.

'What is the matter with you?' he asked.

'Nothing,' she said, 'only I am so weary. Father tires me.'

'Then why complain of a little diversion?' he said testily. 'Do you know what it will be like? Far grander than anything you've ever seen. How can you be so dull?'

She sighed and leaned against him, putting her arms about him lightly. 'Don't be quarrelsome,' she said.

He laughed shortly.

'It isn't that I don't want to go to Ellwin,' she said, moving away from him and looking out on the empty weathering lawn. 'But you frightened me. What did he mean? Why do I have to see William?' Her voice sharpened. 'Why now? It's too soon.'

'But Belle,' he said, 'you're not a child. Look at yourself.' He followed her and stood close, putting a note of jovial admiration into his voice. 'Is it any wonder Harlock wants you for his son. And in any case—'

'I don't want to marry William,' she said bluntly, like a child saying it doesn't want porridge. She turned again as if his prox-imity irked her, and again he followed. He watched her watch-ing the hawk. Phoebe stretched her legs, one then the other, then the broad, powerful wings in like fashion. Belle was cold. The bones of her face were thin ice thinly covered. He pitied her. The child would eat the porridge and she would have William. He kissed the bone ridge above one eye.

'You will come home whenever you want to,' he said pleas-antly.

She frowned, moving her shoulders impatiently.

'Listen,' he went on, putting a comforting arm about her shoulders, 'it is so close and I will be there so often, and you here, you'll scarcely notice a difference.'

She scowled as if he'd offered her a hovel, pushing him away and reeling back so hard that she hurt her arm against the door frame, before running out into the yard with a smothered cry.

He watched her go, running blindly with her head down and the yellow veil trailing from her fingers. He felt sick. Something was terribly wrong with her and it was not his fault. Why push at him like that? What was he, some dolt, some pig?

He straightened and returned to his hawk, his face burning, sitting still and waiting for the mews to work on him again.

here are too many on the move.'

Harlock had the air of a man perplexed by some injustice. His wide brow wrinkled as he sucked the sauce from a peacock's leg, and his eyes had a wounded look. The board cloth, white and crisp when the feast began, was soiled and sticky about him, and the sleeve of his black velvet gown had soaked up a small lake of wine.

He'd had his say. Any man with sense would agree. Only his wife quibbled a little, leaning her large bulk forward and talking across him from time to time in a most irritating fashion to Hugh Rennock, as if she understood or had anything of consequence to add, when it was perfectly obvious that the real burden of the matter escaped her. She was deaf in one ear and missed half of what went on anyway.

'All the same,' she said now, 'it must be very pleasant in the spring.'

'What?' he said, incredulous.

'One sees them sometimes,' she said, 'little children and all. Wandering along gathering ramsons—'

'Absolutely,' said Hugh, inclining his round dark head and smiling. 'As long as the weather is kind. But your husband is right. If it were one or two, forty or fifty even, but we are talking here of a multitude, madam. As for the remedy, I am at a loss.'

May nodded comfortably, watching the antics of a set of fools falling over and over one another in the wide space between the tables. A mummer made filthy gestures at the women.

Harlock snorted. 'I dread the harvest,' he said, drinking deep from a silver cup and closing his eyes. The remedy was obvious. The stocks were always full, also the prisons. More were needed.

Too many of his own breed shrugged and played foul, buying any runaway for better wages than his neighbour and asking no questions. They fuelled a dreadful fire, he was sure. He was very drunk. Opening his eyes on the mirth and brightness of his own hall, it seemed to him that a kind of trembling fell upon the gathered company, dreamlike and momentary. This was his house, insubstantial as the castle of paper, intricately crenellated, that the servants had carried in and set amongst the dishes a short while before. A pall of sound rose and fell dully, settling on his brain like a cloth. Smoke from the torches stilled and thickened in a milling canopy that pressed like poor weather from on high, threatening rain.

'It surely has something to do with the spread of plague,' Hugh Rennock was saying.

'What?' said May.

'Plague, madam. They spread plague.'

'That I *do* fear,' she said.

'It offends against reason.' Harlock felt his worry like an ache in the head. 'They have safe nests. I try to understand. Where are they? Not in the fields, that I know. And more each day, more each day! Aye, there are good and bad masters, but enough is enough. Sim! Where is he? Do we have dancers? I've had my say. I say, I have had my say. Aye, I know what I would do with them.'

They would fall like the falls of frogs and fishes one heard of, a deadly shower from the sky—haggish women and brutish men, stinking of filth, drowning in a flood of ordure this bright company, every bright company. The threat made him burn with anger, and he damned the wretched lot of them and hoped they got corns and boils and worms and the plague itself, and that the weather would turn cold and soak them through wherever they tried to sleep.

'The sadness of it is,' said May, 'that the laws are for their own benefit, but they don't see it.'

'Quite,' said Hugh.

Harlock growled, leaning down to slip a morsel of skin into the soft wet mouth of a young bloodhound. 'This is no time for leniency,' he said, wiping his fingers on his thighs. 'I've had my fill of it. Come harvest, where will we be?'

'What?' said May.

'What? What?' he snapped.

'Don't you chide,' she said indifferently.

On the gallery, the high arched bow of the viol dipped and soared and the music was soothing. Sim appeared at Harlock's elbow. 'My lord,' he said, 'the dancers are ready.'

Harlock turned his head to look at the boy. 'Soon,' he said. Sim withdrew, the perpetual thin crescent of a smile creasing the lower part of his face. His light brown hair was smooth and polished as an acorn. Harlock softened, leaning back replete, searching his teeth with his tongue and listening with easing pleasure to the singing of a man with a voice like cream, telling of a woman whose lover came headless home.

'William sings like that,' May said. 'Does he not?'

Harlock looked at his son, a sweet, milky boy with a hanging lip, sharing a platter with Rennock's sister, whose stemlike neck and arrogant bearing he was beginning to find as irksome as his son's pale spirit. Oh, she would do. She was fair, clear of the pox, well-dowried. William presented her courteously with a dish of sugared plums. She smiled briefly, shaking her head. The two of them lacked choler and sat there in a kind of lumpen fog, as if the celebration, music, mirth and all were some faintly trying aberration. Harlock's chin tightened sardonically.

Three or four young hounds began to quarrel and snap. Without ceremony Sim hauled the creatures apart. William watched, his blue eyes anxious as his darlings were cuffed. Dogs were to him as dolls to a girl. Harlock watched him call Sim and remonstrate, saw Sim nod compliantly then turn away and make droll mouths at the cautiously sniggering servants. His face was made for foolery.

We should have swapped them at birth, thought Harlock guiltily. I could have done it too if only Sim had come to us in time. One's very like another when they're babes, she'd never have noticed.

A falcon cried out from the rafters. Hugh Rennock looked towards the sound, raising the wine cup to his lips with shining eyes. Or him, thought Harlock, growing melancholy now as wine and music mingled in his mind. Hugh would have made a good son. It should be his own flesh sitting here beside him, a fine hearty young man, bone of his bone, blood of his blood, the kind he'd fought beside in his youth. He remembered—he always remembered—the danger, the strong valour like sap rising in a young tree, the smell of mud and blood, men's eyes staring mad, and all the world confined in his body with the singing nerves. Good memories. What had he now? Only the chase, and the dreary struggle to find labour enough to work his land.

In the armoury he had a collection to rival any—knives, swords, axes, helmets, shields—wonderful, beautiful things from the deep corners of the world. They sang of battle; deep, hot battle, horrible, roaring, worthy of heroes. Harlock felt warm and mellow. Rennock, he thought, had some fine nervous quality. He must show him the armoury. Better still, make him a gift. Of course, the outlaw's knife, it was perfect, a treasure—the shining double-edged blade, thin like a murderous bone, the handle styled like two fishes, the sheath like a shell, very finely tooled in leather. From melancholy he passed to smiling fondly on the entertainment before him. They'd taken the outlaw near Ellwin Beck last year in the snows. Now how, he thought, did a wretch like that come by such a knife? A filthy brute of a dog he was, with a face like stone, but his bowed legs quaked when they bound him in a cart and rattled him away to the gallows. Something always gave them away, some twitch, some smell, and they never looked you in the eye. It was a rare pleasure these days, he thought, to watch a man die, and the thought surprised him.

They were singing a new song of Bayardine. Enough, he thought, time for the dancers. But he let them continue, splaying his big hands upon his belly and assuming a serious air as he listened:

> 'It was not for the good red gold
> Nor yet for meat and wine,
> But all was for an elfin grey
> Some men call Bayardine.'

Beside him his wife leaned forward, smiling, enchanted. Her face, round and fair and forthright, was sweating slightly through the fine white dust with which she coated it, and her throat blossomed beneath her chin in a pale soft curve reminiscent of the crop of a dove. When he looked at her, desire mixed with contempt.

He blew his nose loudly into his hand and wiped it on his clothes, then made a show of boredom, picking his teeth with his long horny nails. Fools, he thought. Let some half-wit run wild and they rave of murder. Let him show his face at a window at night, they rave of ghosts. Let him be a witch's whelp of monstrous size, the mark of the flames he fled on his ugly face, they rave of fiends that lift their own from the fire, dark courts that give him refuge, bargains with the devil.

And we have one more outlaw. They're worse than the runaways, they come out of the forest like maggots from a cheese at night. He's one of them if he's alive, and he's subject to death.

The song ended and he called for the dancers.

You will be rich, Hugh had said. You will live at Ellwin Hall.

Live here? With these people, this husband? Well, she could eat at least. She'd filled the trencher again and again, hoping they'd think her too gluttonous for their finicky son, sitting there beside her with his fingers scarcely soiled. She'd never seen so many different kinds of meat and fowl and fish, so many sauces and sweets and dainties, and she had to try them all. Now the strong wine had gone to her head and her wits danced with the pipes and drums, making her smile in a foolish way.

But she hated the place. She had shivered coming under the big stone arch where the unicorns ramped and a lion faced an eagle, through the gloomy courtyard and into the great echoing house of high rooms and heavy doors, narrow staircases that curved away into flickering darkness, footfalls and voices heard in distant chambers. Home was so much smaller and warmer. The first thing she had noticed was the smell of new rushes covering another, less pleasant smell, sweet and rotten. May had greeted her, smiling readily, the flesh beneath her pale eyes folding in welcome. Belle was grateful for the warmth of the woman.

'You are so like your mother,' May had said, embracing her. She was quick and plump and peculiarly girlish. 'Is she not? Is she not, my dear?'

Belle was wearing her mother's jewels. Everyone kept saying how she looked like her mother, and she had to keep smiling pleasantly. Sometimes she felt as if the shade of her mother sat upon her shoulders, grinning out like a gargoyle over her head.

She drank some more, tilting her head back rather grandly and toying with her mother's brooch, a stag's head in silver with a small ruby at the tip of each antler. It was very old and one of the antlers bent away slightly between her restless fingers. I could break this very easily, she thought, taking a sideways look at William, who hadn't spoken for a long time and now sat in a state of awkwardness so profound that it set around him like jelly. The poor harmless thing, she thought. Marry him? She was cold. The smoke stung her eyes and the fire roared, and fat yellow flames went rushing up the great chimney, but a vicious chill crept from somewhere and made her legs ache. Marry him?

Someone placed a pyramid of nuts and fruit on the trestle and she began to nibble idly, fiddling with the brooch and watching the dancers, whose bones, it seemed, were made of green twigs and bent them into fantastical postures; and watching also certain fragrant, painted young men with their summer-meadow tunics and pointed shoes, their elegant sleeves trailing in the dirt, till, unable to deny the thought further, she painted in the midst of all this a picture of John Heron in his muck and his old grey clothes and wondered how he'd look if his mouth were painted scarlet, like theirs.

She laughed.

Someone breathed familiarly by her neck and she smelt wine and spices. She turned her face to a face with upturned lip and upturned nose and bright, insolent eyes. The face was so close and smiled so knowingly, as if it knew her mind, that she gasped and tightened her fingers on her mother's brooch, breaking an antler from the stag's head and pricking her palm.

'Ypocras, lady,' said Lord Harlock's boy, and poured.

e followed the pale light of a horn lantern through the pitchy night. A small breeze stirred the edge of the forest from time to time, as if the trees heaved faint moaning sighs in their sleep.

Hugh hated his own furtiveness and the fear in his bones. He could not see his feet and stumbled often, cursing silently at the rattling of stones. Belle was too far ahead to notice. He was cold and tired and his eyes felt wide in the dark like the eyes of an owl. Now I know that she's mad, he thought. Where is she going? Unnatural.

The light vanished in the Sallow Meadow. He quickened his pace and his fear quickened with it, and he ran up the last part of the rise and found himself falling headlong, so that his teeth burned and his heart was jolted. God curse the night and all its demons. He sat up, getting his breath and brushing down his clothes, moved almost to tears like a fallen child, disturbed by the uncommon emotion. Then he rose to his feet and drew from its sheath the knife that Harlock had given him.

The light seeped dully from the crack at the side of the door of an old barn across the meadow, one he often rode by during the day. He approached softly, stood at the door and listened. There was no sound. It might have been empty and this the door to a world of nothing that had swallowed her as a toad swallows a fly. A little feeling of dread licked his belly and he put his eye to the crack: nothing.

He must go in. Foolishly, he considered knocking. A terrible urge to laugh overwhelmed him and he turned away, doubling over and sinking to his knees in the dirt as if he had a pain in his gut. Then he rose, steeled himself and stood paralysed, waiting. Burst in on her, fool, go on. But what would she say? Once he'd

26 ❖

come upon her all alone at the end of the garden, talking to the wall as if it had sense. 'What are you spying on me for?' she'd snapped. 'Stop following me about.' And then she'd looked at him as if he was a snotfaced child at the roadside and she a great lady. 'Away and scratch,' she'd said, pushing him lightly.

Sometimes he hated her. She'd taken herself away from him so slowly that he hadn't even noticed, and she made him feel lumpish, crude, backward.

See a little more first, he thought.

He prowled about the walls of the barn trying to see in, finding only a few chinks that revealed no more than the edge of a sickly glow. She's in there with a lover, he allowed himself to think. It made him hot. No, no, she was innocent, she wouldn't be such a fool, and anyway, who did she meet? We've let her alone too much, he thought. It was damnably quiet.

Then he heard a sound like some beast turning over. It made him sweat suddenly, as if ill.

And after, unmistakably, the muted sounds of heated fornication.

Hugh walked back to the road very quickly, and on till he reached a bank of bushes, where he rested and hid, his head upon his knees and his arms enclosing all. After a while he looked up. His eyes were growing accustomed to the dark or it was getting lighter, because he could see where the bushes ended and the sky began. He felt dirty. His face burned. He felt strangely like the timid mongrel bitch his father kept, the one that trembled and cowered when the great hounds committed canine sins, as if the faults were all her own. He started to laugh, covering his mouth with his hand as if to keep it in, shaking and spluttering and gasping for air. Fool! he thought. Hiding! From what? Who is there to see? And he stood up, defiant, a grin upon his face.

Immediately the madness passed and he was grim. He must

act. He stood tense, growing colder, a bitter taste in his mouth.
He should go up there now, break the infernal door and walk
in, thrash the beast senseless as he lay across her—

He swallowed.

—naked, they'd both be naked, and he allowed himself to
imagine it, her and him, the unknown him, and there in his
mind he saw that the naked man was himself, and gave a start.
He put his head in his hands, lust growing, tears starting in his
eyes. He should have stayed in his bed. He should be home now,
sleeping, safe. None of this was true. She was innocent. She was
marrying William, and sometimes he would ride out to see her
and they would sit together and talk very pleasantly of her
childhood and his youth. True, all of it, and she was in the barn
with a beast.

He started up the road towards the Sallow Meadow grimly.
Nearing the barn it occurred to him that she would scream
when he threw back the door. Would she beg him, terror in her
eyes? Would she, naked? What then? His throat was tight. He
would not hurt her. But him. Him. There would be blood. His
grip tightened on the handle of the knife. Kill him. Mark him.
Spoil his face. Fillet his pintle. What will she do? Beg for him?
Hate me? Hate me?

There was no sound. He stood outside the door for a long
time.

Suppose he's a lord, he thought. Someone greater than me.
Suppose, even, it was William—no, impossible. Still he stood,
till his heart had calmed down and he could breathe sanely.

He thought he saw a way to save her, to save himself, to
unmake all that had happened, and none to know but he and
she, a secret that would bind them together.

He stood debating with himself. A night bird called.

There was a stirring in the barn. He withdrew amongst the
sallow bushes. Light was growing over the forest. She came out,

he saw her hand upon the fold of her mantle for a second before she set off home, walking quickly with head bowed and the hood pulled down over her face.

He did not move. He was a shadow, a bush. Birds would come and nest in him.

A young man in peasant clothes appeared in front of the barn and stood for a moment looking this way and that, moving his shoulders and taking the fine morning air, like a man just stepping out for a piss. Hugh's brain clenched. The knife stirred. The man walked down the hill towards Caddenhope, out of sight.

Hugh stood looking at the knife in his hand. The birds were beginning to sing. Not a lord then. It was the fellow who ploughed for his father. He'd spoken to him once or twice, a cocky little churl with a winning smile, big teeth in a bonny brown face.

Big white teeth could be broken.

Hugh sheathed the knife and went home.

'I saw you,' he said.

It was nearing prime. She stood in the hall by the parlour door, about to go in to their father.

'I saw you,' he said again softly from the foot of the stairs.

'Saw what, Hugh?' she said absently.

'I couldn't remember the name at first. Then it came to me. John Heron.'

She looked at him blankly.

'There is a law against it. Didn't you know?'

'What?' she whispered. 'What?'

'Whoring,' he said, trying not to blink.

She looked sick with fear. She walked a few steps towards him, eyes downcast, then sank upon the stairs with her hands clasped in her lap. He stood looking down on the crown of her head and the steep slopes of her shoulders. Her jaw moved, as if she were grinding her teeth very slowly.

'Belle,' he said, sitting down beside her, 'look at me.'

She covered her face.

'Belle,' he said patiently.

'No.' Her voice was muffled.

He tried to take her hands from her face but she pulled violently away, turning to the wall as if it could offer shelter.

'I know everything,' he said, 'I was there. You were in the barn in the Sallow Meadow and—'

She shuddered, then beat her fists on her knees. He caught sight of her face all swollen and childish, though there were no tears. She tried to speak but no words came.

'Belle,' he said sorrowfully (how gentle I am, a gentle brother), 'Belle, what have you done? What have you—'

'How dare you!' she whispered, fixing her hands around his arms like claws and digging in with her nails. She spoke with great precision and controlled fury straight into his face, staring into his eyes. 'How dare you follow me! How dare you creep and spy and—' She let him go as if he stank, turning away with a strangled cry and bending double. For a moment he thought she would vomit on the stairs.

Her rage fuelled his own. She is foul and sullied and she speaks so to me, he thought, and he gripped her as she had him, frightening her with the suddenness of the change, shouting into her face so that her eyes blinked. 'Have you no sense at all? If it were known! How can you even bear to think of it? Think, you fool, think! Suppose there were a child, suppose—'

'Sh!' she hissed. 'He'll hear.'

'He won't.' But he lowered his head until it touched hers, and his voice, which trembled and grew thick. 'I can't believe this. Not you, Belle! Belle, I can't bear that any harm should come to you. Don't you know what you risk? If it were known, Belle, if it were known!'

She started to cry.

'Don't you know,' he said, 'he's forever in the ale-house in Caddenhope, pouring gallons down his gullet. Hasn't he a voice? Are you mad? Do you want the lowest—'

'He is not,' she said.

'Belle!' their father called. He'd been purged and bled that morning and a servant was with him.

'It may be too late,' he said.

'He doesn't talk,' she replied hopelessly, 'he wouldn't.'

Hugh laughed. 'Oh, he's too *honourable*, is he? A lad like that? Too *noble?*'

She smeared her face, a dreadful grin of misery distorting her features. 'Why not?' she said. 'Why can't he be honourable?' But the anger was all gone and she dripped water. It works, he thought, a sense of power creeping through him quietly. I have her now.

'Oh, Belle!' he said, full of sympathy and regret. 'Oh, Belle! Is that what you believed? Of course you did.'

'What shall I do?' she gasped. 'What shall I do? Am I damned? Am I damned? Oh, Hugh, I am damned, I am damned, I am damned!' Her fear took away her voice and gave her face a haggard, albino look.

'Belle!' called Rennock.

'I have to go to Father,' she whispered. 'What can I do?'

He looked at her. See, his eyes said, how very much I care for your well-being, how nearly I weep for your trouble. And how I understand! He drew her close and laid her hot face against his chest, one hand gently caressing the back of her head. 'Don't cry,' he said. 'Would I let any harm come to you? Now, Belle! What do you think? Sh! Quiet and think. Who knows about this?'

'Only you and I,' she said, blowing her nose.

(You and I and John Heron.)

'Listen,' he said, putting her from him a little and speaking sternly. 'It's over. You see that? It's madness and it's over. Now it has to be as if it never happened and in a little while you will believe it. No-one else will know a thing.'

This brought on more crying.

'If he speaks,' said Hugh, 'no-one will believe him.' He gestured as if it were self-evident: 'the drunken bragging of a fool.'

'He will not speak,' she said sharply, and went on angrily, her face blank: 'I knew it was impossible. I'm not such a fool as to think otherwise. He'll come to the barn and he'll wait and I'll not come and he'll think—'

'He'll think nothing,' Hugh said, letting a little impatience creep into his voice. 'I know these lads. I know this one by reputation. I marked him down for a runaway long ago. Any day now he'll up stakes and be off. Oh, you must have known it! Didn't he run away from some other manor to come here—' Something glimmered in his mind, some seed put forth a shoot. 'Isn't this true?'

She looked away. True, he'd come from the sea. She'd never seen the sea. He said it was as big as the forest. He loved to talk. His mother wore a liripipe and pounded something in a tub the day he left home. She did not even look round. She looked like a man, he said, she was starting a moustache.

'And what will she do without you?' Belle had asked.

'Well enough,' he'd said cheerfully. 'She's plenty more.'

'You are not to think of him any more,' Hugh said.

That was impossible.

'It is impossible,' he said. 'Everything is impossible. He has nothing in the world.'

'He has a parsley patch,' she said.

THE UNMAKING ❖ 33

There was silence for a moment, then Hugh laughed. 'A parsley patch,' he repeated. It was all nonsense. Suddenly he roared with laughter. 'A parsley patch! Ellwin Hall! Ellwin Hall for a parsley patch!'

Surprised, Belle laughed too but cried again immediately. 'It's your fault,' she said. 'A good man's a good man. That's what you taught me. What about the Gospels on the wall? The poor are better than the rich, and we should envy them.'

Hugh laughed still. 'You are right, of course. What are we to think? Should we not all fling off our things like poor friars? We are not friars, Belle! We're flesh and blood. You misunderstand and take things too far. Have sense, girl, have sense. The world would come crashing down if—'

'I don't know how I am to live now!' she cried out suddenly, jumping up and looking round distractedly. He was very sorry for her and very happy suddenly. She was looking at him, bereft, and he saw himself—strong, loyal, gentle, sitting on the stairs with a certain grace. 'Everything will be just the same,' he said, 'in time.'

'Will it?' she said earnestly. 'Will it? And will you promise—'

'Belle!' their father called.

'You are very good!' she said.

He smiled. 'You think you will never forget,' he said. 'Wait. When you are a married lady living at Ellwin—'

It was a mistake.

'No,' she said flatly. 'I won't marry William. There is no question of it. My mind is made up.'

His anger surprised him. He had shown such tolerance and kindness, far more than she deserved. She was a fool.

'Oh, but you will,' he said dangerously. 'This is too much. You *are* mad.'

She screamed and stamped her foot.

'It is final,' he said.

She flew into their father's room in tears and threw herself down on the bed, sending the white cat hurtling. 'Father!' she pleaded, 'Tell him! I don't have to marry William if I don't want to, do I? You said. You said it would be my decision in the end. Please. Tell him.'

Hugh stood scowling in the doorway. The room smelt of excrement. The servant discreetly withdrew. Rennock's face was the colour of faded lilacs, patched with primrose under the eyes. It hovered like a thin, sick moon amongst the bed clothes. A thin hand came from somewhere and touched her head.

'Don't taunt your sister,' he said mildly.

'Father,' said Hugh, 'they have been betrothed since she was an infant.'

'I don't care!' she cried. 'I refuse!'

'Belle,' said the old man kindly, 'now, dry your face, child. Of course we won't make you do anything you don't want to.'

He signalled the opposite to Hugh, waving a hand for peace. Hugh turned and left the room. He felt like leaping, pulling faces, whooping through his cupped hands. He itched with power. But it was not over. What must he do? Lie down and gather his racing wits, think calmly. Phoebe. He would go to the mews and gaze into her wild yellow eye and then he would know what it was he had to do, what the shoot meant, unfurling from the seed in his mind.

But the mews would stifle him. He needed air. He called instead for Serafina and rode as hard as he could to the top of the ridge that rose up between Caddenhope and the road to Ellwin. There he turned his horse and looked back at the land that was his father's and would soon be his. They were out in the fields, the grey figures walking, bending, wielding tools that might be weapons. Directly beneath him a man walked slowly, casting seed out of a bag that hung down from his neck, left, right, left, right, an easy rhythm.

Soon he was calm.

She's ruined. She'll fall again.

John Heron has defecated on holy ground.

The seed went into the ground and he felt the seed in him. It was growing. He felt it. It ached and made him feel a little sick. He licked his dry lips and tried to ignore it but it blossomed, not a plant but a worm probing through his brain, which whirled madly, as if all in a second the worm had given birth to a clot of lively offspring.

'Oh, God,' he whispered. 'Oh, God.'

ohn Heron was afraid. His upper lip sweated and his eyes waited for clues. The man looked him over. It was her brother. He commanded John to leave off scraping the dirt from a harness, to put by his knife and accompany him; his man was sick, he said, and he had need of an assistant to carry for him. A fierce bright hawk, unsummed, sat upon his wrist, her fearful claws biting the glove.

'I'll give you good wages,' Hugh said, his heels teasing the sides of the powerful grey mare, which danced a little backward and shook her mane.

John laid the harness down. The bird bated, flinging herself forward. He flinched slightly. Hugh laughed. John laughed too, foolishly.

'She is too keen,' Hugh said as he settled her once more, stroking her breast and crop lovingly. 'Ah, she will not always allow this. There, my love! Phoebe! We should see good sport. The day is perfect. She's at her best weight.'

Then he laughed again, as if some happiness in him was too great to contain, smiling down pleasantly at John. Fine legs and shoulders, yes, he thought. Face fair and round. Filthy little tyke. He's wondering. Look at his eyes. The eternal peasant's, ready to cloud over or beg at a word.

'Come,' he said heartily, pulling on the rein.

The mare's great flanks swayed. John walked at the stirrup-foot, carrying a bag that jogged against his right side. He doesn't know, John thought. How can he? Someone has told him I'm a good man, strong, reliable. That's it. He's one of those that speaks very fair and free to my sort, man to man, you might say. The common touch. You still have to mind your lip. Not like her. Not at all. She was unlike the rest. He knew she was dangerous. He'd known it long before she spoke to him. It was just as stupid as falling in love with the lady in the great painting on the wall of the church at home, in the chancel where he was not allowed. A Saint, that one, nothing touched her, certainly not he. Sin even to think it, he supposed, though he did, many times during a long sermon with the flies buzzing and the crowd stinking and the sun flaming in through the high windows like fire on his head. It was the same with Belle. She had no right at all to look at him, nor he to look back. Gentry women often stared, that was not new; but she had looked again and again, smiling sadly and frankly straight into his eyes, as if she wished him to understand something about her that words were not permitted to say. He'd always been a fool. Months had passed, and he watched for her. Fool. He saw it and he glowed and it seemed that the harsh edges of his life were softened. Then he was plunged into sadness so deep and threatening that he thought of going away, but didn't, and she went on passing, smiling now, and he smiled back, knowing that his smile was charming, threw a graceful languor over his movements when-ever she appeared, straightening his shoulders and letting the lids of his eyes fall softly, slowly. He was good at this. And then she spoke, alighting from her horse and standing picking at the reins, asking him about the oxen—had they names and were they very tired and what did he say to them, and when he answered she listened so closely that he began to think his words were pearls.

And both of them were netted, all without a word.

'We will turn aside here,' said Hugh. There was a tussocky field bordered by low scrub. John hefted the bag. Still, deep inside his body, he was afraid. Oh, but the man is so friendly, he thought. She says he's a good man. Wonder what he'd do if he knew what I have in my pocket?

Wrapped in a dock leaf there, he held one ruby-tipped silver antler. A ruby, she had given him a ruby.

PHOEBE'S eye flamed and her thighs clenched. Her mail was ruffled and some great rage seemed pent within her. Not far from the forest's edge a big brown buck rabbit with a noble nose started up before them. Hugh felt the cruel claws tighten on him like the grip of fear, pricking his senses, whetting him like a knife. His arm began to rise slowly, too slow, she was gone, not quite upon the buck, which streaked away and put in at a nearby brake. The bird flew, her jesses trailing. She rose a little, sailed, settled into her flight with beating wings vigorously moulding the air. She was so beautiful tears came to his eyes. His lips drew back. She went away flying low, rose, floated on the sky as if it were fine blue silk, then banked so that they saw her pale underparts.

John helped him serve her. The buck broke cover. She came in sideways, swift and deadly, killing in a second, the bells on her feet ringing as she clutched, crumbling bone. Death's Angel, pure and lovely. The juices spirted in Hugh's mouth.

She was given the buck's head.

They went into the forest a little way. It was cool and peaceful, full of pleasant dappling movement. The green roof twinkled. The going was hard for John, his thin shoes poor protection on the track they followed, which was hard and stony and fretted with shallow roots. More than once he stumbled. The buck grew heavy in the bag that banged at his side and the smell of fresh blood came up into his nostrils.

Further in, it grew darker. He kept looking over his shoulder and up to where the sky was hidden, swallowing apprehensively. How did this man know where he was going? He'd never get out of here alone. He thought of all the robbers and cut-throats and lepers and lunatics the forest had swallowed up and wondered what became of them all. Sometimes a bolt of light fell in and the smooth blue sky appeared, held at bay, unutterably distant. Poor John, he thought, and shivered. Poor John. It was what he used to chant to himself as a child, rocking himself into peace in the shelter on days when the wind whistled and his fingers were numb and blue and scarce able to wield the clapper, two hours more to go and a flock of vicious young crows threatening the corn.

But then they came to a clearing surrounded by beech trees, where the earth was thick with mast, fast with the scurrying of ants. Herb Robert and bluebells grew beneath the trees. Here Hugh dismounted, saying it was time for food and drink. 'Then,' he said, fixing his dancing eyes very briefly on John, 'you will see how well she flies in cover.' He stuck his bow in the ground and let the hawk sit there playing with the buck's head, the bell on her tail sounding its gentle discord as she moved. His horse grazed free.

John looked up at the sky and around at the trees. Twilight began all around him. He felt as if he were at the bottom of a well.

Hugh offered him bacon and bread and ale, eating heartily himself and concentrating fiercely on the food. 'Eat,' he said, 'don't pick. What is it? Are you afraid?' He swallowed noisily, wiping his lips with the back of his hand, then leaned forward and smiled in a friendly manner. 'I am sorry,' he said, 'I forget you are not well acquainted with these woods. Not all men are at ease here.' He laughed. 'There is nothing to fear, believe me. We'll go no further in.'

John relaxed a little. The ale was good. 'I am not so afraid, sir,' he said, smiling.

'Of course not,' Hugh said, breaking bread with delicate fingers, very like his sister's. I thought he was not like her, thought John, but there is something. Then Hugh looked up. 'I've heard about you,' he said.

'Sir?' John stiffened.

'My father's well pleased with you. You work hard, he says. Here—' He proffered the horn, brimming with ale. 'Let's not dawdle. Drink. I mean we are aware of the value of good men. Do you understand?'

'I understand.' John was not sure. Is he offering me better wages? he thought.

Hugh's eyes were warm and bright. John allowed his mind to wander. We will become friends, he thought. He will raise me. Serfs have become freemen, freemen may rise, and rise again.

'Herb Robert,' said Hugh eagerly, as if it were something he'd just remembered, 'is very good for disorders of the blood.'

Mistress Heron.

'Here,' said Hugh. He put some bread in his mouth and chewed ebulliently, fishing about amongst his clothes. 'Take my pouch and fill it. Mind you get the flowers too. And leave it open.'

I'll take my sister Belle a nosegay, he nearly said, laughing soundlessly, watching as John walked with the pouch to the shadow of a great beech and there dropped into a squat, contemplating the small purple flowers with his neck thrust forward and his dull brown hair parting about it.

Moving without a sound, Hugh drew his knife and approached him, noting how carefully the dirty fingers nipped the red stems, one by one. He'd never killed in this way before, close and silent. As he struck, the boy moved as if about to turn, aware perhaps of a presence; Hugh's hand weakened and the knife missed its place, penetrating a mere inch or two into the left shoulder and sticking there as if it would never move again. John did not even grunt. He fell sideways with his face in the damp mould.

Oh, Lord God, a paltry blow! Hugh drew in a sharp breath between gritted teeth, cursing himself. It was meant to go home between the shoulder blades, all seven inches. Quick! he thought, press it in, both hands, lean on it, right up to the fish's mouths! But he stood there tranced, closely watching John Heron's face, which frowned stupidly, perplexed. The look changed to one of concentration as his right hand felt for the knife and was arrested half way as if by an invisible grip, groping in air. The left lay useless beneath him.

He seemed to notice Hugh for the first time. A great breath came, as if from a bellows. 'Something struck me,' he said with an idiot's voice.

He had not understood. Now I must kill him, thought Hugh. One blow this time. He felt the hairs on his body prick. John pushed at the ground with his right hand, trying to rise, his face sweating, his feet scrambling madly and failing to get a grip.

Phoebe flew up angrily into a low tree, her bells tinkling.

Hugh stepped forward and plucked out the knife. Blood soaked the grey coat so quickly it shone. He raised the boy briskly, hearing him cry out, placing him with his back against the tree. A sadness fell on him, but there was no help for it. 'What did you think?' he said, vexed. 'What did you think?' John's head tipped back. His throat was so smooth that there was no other way. It was so easy. The blade slit swiftly, gliding, and a thin red line appeared. It thickened.

Hugh walked quickly away and cleaned the knife on a tuft of moss before sheathing it. A strange muted bubbling sound followed him. When he turned John Heron had risen to one knee, listing slightly, both hands bloodied at his throat. He understood now. His eyes on Hugh's were full of fear and a kind of wonder, and his teeth grinned, shining.

'You silly lad!' Hugh cried, ice cold. 'What have you done? Look what you've brought on yourself!'

John opened his mouth very wide. Blood spilled down the front of him. Hope remained in his eyes, and Hugh exploded in fury at such presumption. Men should die when their throats were cut. Hugh turned on the spot, round and round, looking for something to finish it with. There were stones and rocks lying about and he stooped and hoisted a good hefty one and hurled it at John Heron's head. It struck and down he went, lying full-length on his face with his arms outflung. Hugh ran to him, seized the rock and raised it again, beat it twice hard on the back of his head and saw blood begin to seep through the hair.

Enough.

He stepped back, breathing hard, then walked away to the far side of the clearing and stood looking into the darkness. There was no sound. After a while he felt calm enough to return. The body lay as he had left it, blood pooling under the face. He watched it closely for a while then began to turn it with the tip of his boot but stopped immediately, afraid of seeing the eyes. He was not a coward. Blood was nothing. But he was deep in the forest and it came to him unexpectedly that this might annul nature's laws, as if the forest itself was a dream that held him fast. As in a dream, a dead man might rise again. This was fancy, understandable given the circumstance, he told himself. Sometimes fancy needed harsh treatment. He poked and prodded at the body. Nothing stirred. Nearby, open amongst the little purple flowers, those that had been plucked withering already, lay his pouch. He took it up, then stood in silence for a long time until he became aware of a sound like many women whispering in suppressed delight.

Fear dried his mouth. Then he realised it was just the leaves rustling very far above, where a breeze must have started to blow. Looking up, he saw them, light green and transparent against a sky turning cold, and it seemed to him he must have stood there for hours.

The boy was dead.

Hugh turned his head and saw that Serafina, on the far side of the clearing, had stopped feeding to look at him. Dully, he looked back.

Phoebe flew onto a branch close by, making the leaves shake. Startled, he stepped back, his foot skidding a little on the mould. What an eye she had, a raging sun! She shrieked, a dreadful sound that set his teeth on edge. Holding out his left arm in welcome, he called to her, but she roused and ran to the end of the branch, looking down at him in stern judgement.

'Phoebe,' he murmured lovingly.

She took flight into the trees.

He followed, swearing, losing sight of her and thrusting the branches aside, then standing still to listen for the bells. After a while he heard them from the left, a merry jingle, stopping, starting again further away. She was skilled. She could fly through the wood swiftly, aware of no obstruction, while he stumbled after on the forest bed.

He searched and searched and his thoughts tumbled. Where is she? Where is she? Ungrateful! She got the best of everything. Three nights watching with her in the empty mews till she slept before him and he cried for pity. She'd be wild by morning, never come back. What's she got to reproach *me* for? he thought. Has she never killed? He had to die, it was the only way. He polluted. The shame would do for us all.

I could have banished, not killed, him.

He pursed his mouth to whistle but had not the saliva. He stood working his jaws and trying to gather enough on his tongue to wet his lips, but could not. The urge to weep over-whelmed him and he stood looking about with tears in his eyes, seeing stately oaks and the crabbed arthritic fingers of hornbeam. A great root blocked his way, rearing up to form an arch from which dark curtains of moss hung down in tags. Beneath it wild strawberries grew in the rank dampness, and he fell upon them furiously, stuffing his mouth. They were so sharp they bit his tongue, but he went on eating fixedly like a child comforting some hurt with sugar, till they were all gone and he sat back on his heels, amazed at himself.

It was darker than before. There was no sky above, only leaves. The wood was full of the voices of small birds crying danger, hawk, killer. A crow called harshly.

It was late. If Serafina should have strayed!

Hugh turned and ran till he came to where he knew he must find the clearing and Serafina, his own bow, the bag of game, and the body of John Heron grown stiff under the beech tree. There was only dense foliage, brambles, the furrowed patterns of bark, delicately coloured. Cursing, he ran on across a sloping green sward he'd never seen before, crashed down a bank of ferns and on, to where darkness like the darkness of night prevailed under great trees. There he became a child again, begging sweet Christ to protect him, deliver him from this evil forest, from elves and demons and wild beasts with slavering jaws, and from vile Bayardine, if that devil existed. Dead, Harlock said. But what if he were not? Why wasn't he taken and burned with the rest? His face a mask of fire, hating mankind for it. Prince Demon, they say, sucking the strength even from his own kin.

He ran on, forgetting all but himself lost in the wood with night coming on.

Serafina snorted nearby, a lovely long liquid sound. With a sob of relief he broke through undergrowth and fell into the clearing. A gibbous moon hung far above in a dusky sky and the shadows had grown thick, shrinking the space and covering the body of John Heron carefully, considerately. Dispose of it, he thought. Drag it into the bushes. The shadows were black. He peered but could not penetrate them. To hell with it. Leave it to the birds and beasts. If any find it, let them. They won't blame me.

Serafina was bright under the moon. She had raised her head and was watching him, very still. He was struck with the horrible fancy that she would open her mouth and speak to him with a human voice. His hands trembled as he snatched up his bow and the bag, bloody from the buck. Bone crunched underfoot and he cried out.

The buck's head.

His heart hammered furiously as he hoisted the bag, ran to his horse and mounted heavily. She did not deserve the violence with which he turned her, jerking the reins and driving in the spurs.

Mourning his lost hawk, he rode home.

hen the coughing was very bad she took cala-mint tea to her father, hot as he could bear it, then sat for a while watching him sip. The sounds of the household preparing for bed were peaceful. It rained softly.

'Your eyes are red,' he said. 'What ails you?'

'Nothing, Father.'

His cold hand touched hers. 'Your nothings vex me,' he said weakly, blinking tears from his yellowing eyes. 'Make peace with your brother, do. He is only concerned for your happiness.'

Belle said nothing.

'All of us must wed one day,' he said irritably, as if he were speaking of death. 'If you were getting a dotard or an idiot, there might be cause for tears. But William's young and sound . . . Whisht, girl, whisht!'

For she had started crying again, looking down and spreading her lip.

He sighed, rubbing her hand. He was very tired. 'Sit a while,' he said, 'sit a little while. Tomorrow will be fine.' His voice faded. When she looked up he was asleep, breathing steadily. His mouth hung open and his eyelids were raised, giving him a curiously childlike appearance that disturbed her. It did not do to see one's father as a babe. She settled him and drew up the covers to his chin, then went to bed to weep and think about John Heron.

She wondered if it rained where he was and if he were getting wet, if he were indoors or out, sheltering under a bush perhaps or in some barn. That made her think of the barn where they had lain, the lantern flickering, his lips and eyes and flesh. His body was gentle in spite of the heavy, dirty work he did. She was ill. She could not survive. She was damned and filthy and she would risk Hell because of flesh.

Or even just to see him once, distantly, walking in the field behind the plough. But he was gone. Another man drove the oxen. Butterflies tended the ragwort on the little bit of land where he'd grown parsley.

'You did it! You sent him away!' She'd shouted it.

'Belle, I swear, I swear to you on our Mother's grave I did no such thing. Look at me, look at me. I will not lie. I would have moved Heaven and Earth to stop you from seeing him again, I would have traded my birthright for his solemn vow that he would depart from here and never show his face within a hundred miles. I admit to this. But there was no need. He was a runaway, Belle. I always knew him for a runaway.'

Her tears had obscured her brother's face.

'I swear,' he'd said, 'by all that I hold dear. By the Blessed Virgin and her child, Jesus, the Son of God, I did not banish John Heron.'

He would not risk damnation. That was for her. She'd blinked and Hugh's face had come clear, the eyes soft. She'd needed comfort and held out her hands to him, and he took them. 'It's over,' he'd said. 'It was a nightmare, now you are awake. It did not happen.'

'But I'll not marry,' she had said.

And they had argued again.

There was a ringing in the rain, like bells. She raised her head to listen, but there was nothing. Her own mind made fancies these long, sleepless nights. The bells rang for runaways, out on the long rutted roads where they walked one pace ahead of the statutes, their thin shoes soaking up the wet, their poor heads bowed. For John, gone without a word. Had he looked back from the top of the ridge? Was he thinking about her now? Or was he talking, telling, crowing of her lust and all she'd done, laughing in some stinking tavern with a crew of roaring dolts, their foul red faces slimy with sweat. Go on, go on, and what did she do then? And then? And then, and then? And she a grand lady! A great laugh rose to her window, finding her out. She shuddered, tossing from one side to the other and stifling a groan. Betrayed. Gone for better wages. Money called and he threw her away. Gone.

No. She sat up, wiping her face, sitting very still until she was calm. That he was gone was true. That he had changed his nature was not. Perhaps he thought to save her soul by leaving like this, giving her no chance to change his mind. These people were different, mysterious, she could not tell his motives. But he was not cruel, she knew he was not. The comfort of hating him was denied her.

She lay down and closed her eyes and revelled in remembrance.

An hour later a servant woke her to say that her father was dying, and she rose and dressed and ran shivering down to his room, still dreaming. Hugh was there. Rennock lay still, a flicker in his pale eyelids, a crucifix between his fingers. The priest was called and he was shriven and died, and nothing changed, not so much as the look on his face or the cold in the bones of her feet or the faces of the servants or the sound of the rain.

Hugh wept.

'Belle,' he said, jolting her with his suffering, 'Belle, he's dead, he's dead!' Then he asked her to forgive him.

'What are you talking about?' she asked distantly, a little frown, as of forgetfulness, furrowing her brow. My father lay dying while I rolled in the mud like a sow, she was thinking. While I slobbered on my pillow, pretending it was my lover's face. The bells. The bells rang his soul away, and I thought of lust.

Life was short. Hugh was talking. Life was short, he was

saying. There must be no division between us. Father would have hated it. 'Forgive me,' he repeated. 'Say you believe I had no part in John Heron's leaving.'

'What does it matter?' she said. 'He's gone.'

'But say!'

'I believe you,' she said. 'We'll speak no more of it.'

He kissed her hands. The long dark brows were twisted over his eyes and his tears wet her knuckles, burning hot.

It rained for three days and nights.

On the night after her father's funeral, unable to bear the dim quiet of the house any longer, she stole outside and wandered aimlessly, breathing the sweet moist air and closing her eyes, weaving this way and that, down to the edge of the forest. Dusk would fall soon. The leaves dripped.

The smell of the wet forest excited her.

Dressed all in black, she felt like a stranger in her own body. Under her mantle she'd carried all day a yellow silk veil, a pretty gossamer thing that reminded her of a time she thought must once have existed, when she was young and innocent, slept sound at nights and woke early. She couldn't remember how long ago that was. She wound the veil in and around her fingers constantly, sometimes draping it about her neck and nuzzling at it pruriently, kissing it and pressing it to her nose to sniff the faint perfume of lavender that it held. Though its time was gone, it did not smell of death.

She stood very still. The forest was like a great beast crouching at her back, horribly wild but beautiful, compelling her to plunge her foolish hands into its reeking mane and take the consequences. The smell was heady. Its voice was altogether gentle, compounded of a million tiny droplets of water, a million whispers, the peaceful settling of a million ancient boughs as night prepared to fall. She turned and peered, half fearful, half daring, into its darkening mystery.

How wonderful it would be to walk now into the forest and leave her life behind.

She ventured in a very little way then drew back, breathless. She did this several times. There was a kind of madness in her that she welcomed even as she shrank from it. It must be wrong, this feeling of cold elation. She did not know why. Then she remembered that her father was dead and she in mourning, and she turned back and started walking slowly towards her home.

Unaware of her, a large brown hare crossed the fields towards Caddenhope, stopping and rising to its haunches to look about, ears erect, thin legs poised. It was proud, surveying the land like a lord his demesne, at ease in the gathering blue of dusk. I could be a wolf, she thought, or a hound, or a hawk. I'd be on it in a second. Death was like that. One step and it had you. Though it had not come for her, she thought that it had shown itself in a glass, touching her wrist for a second, whispering: here is a foretaste, Belle, dear. You have many years left. All that you have ever known and loved you must leave now, though you will stay alive. That too is a kind of death.

The hare ran home. She walked on. Nearing the cinder path, she realised she had lost her yellow veil and half turned as if to run back for it. But darkness had fallen on the forest. She shook her head and continued on her way, knowing she would never find it, that it was gone now as her father was gone, as John Heron was gone, as all her life up to this moment was gone. She felt nothing. That would come later.

She would be married to William and live at Ellwin Hall. She would grieve more for John Heron than for her father. Perhaps she would live to be very old. A desert stretched before her, cold under the stars.

After that, Hell's fire.

ime had not yet begun and thick darkness covered everything. Something distant surged like a sea.

That was all.

The creature had floated here forever, sometimes borne up on powerful currents, sometimes hurled so low so fast that its destruction seemed inevitable. Each time it rose again.

It became aware that it had been here for eternity. Then time began.

It became aware of paralysis. Then substance began, and terror, and striving to be born, and pain began, and the world turned over.

Sound became rambling threads that joined and separated, on and on, rising and falling and stopping and starting and moving the darkness before them, becoming at some point voices speaking nonsense.

A dull light glowed.

He thought he was a grub trussed in a spider's web. The pain spread slowly, increasing, filling the body and brain of the grub, which stiffened and formed limbs, becoming in one moment of shock a human creature. The pain was screaming but it made no sound.

A thin black cat with pale green eyes stared impassively, the vibration of its throat visible, the sound a silken thread. There was smoke, it seemed, and a sickening aroma that stuck in the throat. He tried to lift his head and the vision vanished.

'He's awake,' a voice said.

The place was dim, full of grey cloud in which the red of a fire glowed like hell in a shallow pit. There was a roof of rushes.

The head of an ancient woman, wimpled and tortuously wrinkled, appeared in the air. Her long shapeless lips were fierce, clamped one to the other, and the polished beak of a nose was birdlike. He quaked. She spoke. A dark cavern gaped behind the lips. He did not understand and closed his eyes.

When he returned she was still there, now with a body of rags and sticks. A moon-faced boy peered over her shoulder. 'What do you think?' the boy asked. 'Did it work?'

'It worked,' she said.

She gestured and the boy went away. Then she reached down from a great height and touched his face briefly, and he saw that her fingernails caved in, deeply ridged like a ploughed field. The boy returned with a small pot that steamed with the stench he had awoken to. He wanted to turn inside out and hide. 'Hush,' she said, though he'd made no sound. She stirred and mashed, muttering and champing. Astonished, he watched her lips. They were like two worms. Each could not be still at the touch of the other.

'A cloth,' she said.

The boy vanished and reappeared with a grey cloth in his fist, smiling cheerfully down over her shoulder, his hair another moon, black and crescent. 'Don't you fret about the stink,' he said jovially. 'You'll do well enough now.'

Me. He is talking to me.

'Hold your tongue!' said the woman disagreeably, smearing foul brown paste from the pot onto the cloth. Then her hands, swift and terrible, came down to his throat and peeled from there the warm skin, which squirmed and became fat and solid in her fingers, leaving cold nakedness behind for no more than a second before she covered it with the vile slimy plaster. She wound a long red band round and round his neck, the boy supporting his head and shoulders.

'Someone did a very poor job,' she said grimly.

'Lucky for you,' said the boy, smiling at him as he settled his head. 'I'm called Rawl. I found you. Lucky for you, eh?'

'Get rid of this,' said the old woman, scowling. In her hand she held the mess she'd ripped from his throat. It looked like old meat. The boy took it and went, lifting a sack from a low doorway through which he passed into green daylight.

For a moment she looked down at him. Then her face came very close, unsmiling. 'This is the fifth day,' she said, nodding once, sagely, like God announcing a stage of creation. And with that she rose, shook her skirt and straightened her grimy wimple and followed the boy.

He lay on a bed of straw in a small hut lit by one sunken window in the mud wall. Smoke bunched there in its eagerness to escape. Fleas hopped in the straw and an osier basket stood by the door. His pain span out from him, into the roof and the floor and the walls, outside of which nothing existed. The old woman returned with a bowl and a horn and fed him thin broth from one and strong juice from the other, till the pain abated slowly like the tide going out.

He slept fitfully.

When he awoke the sack had been raised and daylight fell over the threshold. He was alone. The fire burned low and the pain was somewhere far beyond the sea, beckoning. He remembered the cat, the old woman, the boy called Rawl, nothing more. His head ached. Outside he heard voices, the shout of a child. With a shock, he recognised his hands resting before him: good, dear hands, full of scratches that were almost healed. A scar on the mount of Venus in the right one attested to some mishap, but God alone knew what it was. This made him want to stick out his lip and snivel, for he was hopelessly lost and could only mourn himself, a dear friend dead and buried. He put his new-found hands to his face and felt it wonderingly, like a blind man, but the fingers told him nothing. He did not know his own face.

Fear gripped him. He tried to rise but fell back. He tried again, very slowly, first resting on an elbow. A sharp throbbing began in his other shoulder but he managed to sit up, sick and breathless. There was nothing to hold on to so he dropped to his knees on the floor and swam through a dream to the doorway, rested on its raised lip and looked out.

It was a soft spring day. A sweet warm smell of herbage tempered with wood smoke soothed him, making hunger in the pit of his stomach, not alone for food but for freedom from the dingy hut and the smell of his own sick body. A sack of goose feathers had been left by the doorway, and a little further away a bundle of firing.

He was in a forest. The trees had been thinned. Amongst tall trunks of trees he glimpsed rough mud walls and shaggy roofs. Immediately before him was a wide dusty clearing where a low spreading fire of logs burned, ashy round the edges and set about with the thick stumps of trees. A woman in brown sat on the ground beside the fire, shredding parsnips into a cloth. Smoke rose from an old black cauldron that sat crookedly amongst the logs. He could hear its bubbling. The woman's back was bowed and her dirty dark hair hung loose over bare brown arms, muscular and dotted with roseate scabs.

He stared and stared at her arms, hearing voices somewhere, sensing activity. Her arms disturbed him and he closed his eyes. A picture flashed on the darkness for one bright second: the splayed hoof of an animal treading muddy earth. Gone.

He opened his eyes and saw two men standing at rest amongst the trees talking. A tough, sturdy baby in a little woollen dress came hooting like a dove, crawling on naked arms and legs, grey with dust, over the rough ground. Reaching the woman, it pulled itself up by her hair, pushing back her clothing to reveal a long swollen breast. She moved slightly as the child fed, and he saw her face, long-lipped and frowning with deep lines beside the nose. Putting down her knife, she supported the child with one arm, turning her face to the sky with a heavy movement and closing her eyes as if her face were a bowl to catch the rays of the sun.

He looked up. The sky, deep blue with stark white clouds sitting still in it like boats, called into him a feeling of sadness, as if it were something precious he'd once owned and lost and saw now beyond reach. So he climbed up the step and stood in the fresh air, nearer to the sky, which dipped and shuddered as the earth heaved, tipping him over. A stone grazed his cheek and skipped away. He saw a plain of dust spreading out from his eye, heard the babble of a multitude and the sound of running feet. Hands raised him and set him with his back to a stump.

There were faces, all speaking in tongues. A ragged band surrounded him. They stared and he stared.

'Poor lad!' someone said.

An old man's face came closer than the rest, grinning tooth-lessly. 'Well, now,' it shouted, 'soon be chasing the maids again!' and roared with laughter.

Someone offered water but he could not drink.

'Is he healed?' asked a boy.

'Aye, but he'll not speak again,' a voice replied.

Then the old woman herself came flapping through the crowd, beating them back as if they were unruly chickens. 'Away!' she intoned, like doom. 'Does he want to look at your ugly faces? Atonement!' Her finger, long and gnarled, curving down at the tip, quivered at his throat. 'Think on your own Sins! Filth!'

He sickened and swooned. When he revived the crowd was gone but little time had passed, for the fire had neither died nor been fed. The old woman poked in the ashes with a stick, squatting down with her skirts trailing in the dirt. A mist obscured her. A long brindle hound lay on its belly close by, rapturously licking the marrow from a bone held between its feet.

An arm supported his back.

'See that old hag over there?' said a man's voice close by his ear. 'That's Dame Lane. She is your sweet mother now. Twenty-nine at least she's got, what's one more? Hates 'em all so vicious, she can't leave 'em alone. Give her a kiss sometime, why not? Hey? One sweet kiss for a sweet mother's brow.'

It was not mist but smoke, drifting away into the hollows of the forest. A clot of midges fretted on the edge of the trees. He could not turn his head. The supporting arm was withdrawn and he felt wood against his back.

The man appeared before him, sitting on the ground with one arm upon the neck of the hound. The left side of the man's face reminded him of some animal, cunning and playful, small-eyed and curly-lipped with a high cheekbone; the right was three-fourths burned, purple and shiny and cockled. The left eye was mild, the right pierced, hooded by a stray flap of skin. Curling fair hair fell about his face and covered his shoulders and a very fine silver buckle shone at his waist.

'Know me?' he said, grinning a grin that showed his gums. The front teeth were gone and the canines were black at the roots. 'Know me, do you?'

Know him? Should I? I would not forget a face like that?

'False repentance,' said Dame Lane. 'None at all. God knows. God sees. He will come in clouds of glory and burn the stinking lot of you. I have told Him. I have told Him what you do.'

'She's mad,' the man said. 'Can you talk, son?'

'Don't be a fool, Bayardine,' she spat.

'Can't talk then. Can't tell me ought then. Where's the use in that? Where you from, son? What they say about me where you come from? Understand me, yes? Yes? Know who I am? Spawn of Satan, yes, boil on the bum of his lowliest imp, and to add to that . . .'

Surprisingly nimble, the old woman jumped up. She crossed herself like one preparing for battle, then scuttled over and struck Bayardine a resounding blow on the head with the flat of her hand. 'Shame! Shame!' she hissed, and spat again.

Bayardine laughed.

She hurried away, whispering.

'She'll pray for me now,' he said, flouncing his curls with his fingers. 'She loves it. Sin, I mean. The priest told her she was bound for Hell so she took it on herself to finish off what Christ began. We are her apprenticeship. Poor old chuck, she's a passenger for Heaven, more like.' He stood up, seizing a burned-out stick from the edge of the fire, and the hound leapt to its feet, abandoning the bone. The man was tall, big-boned and loose-limbed, with large hands and feet and a sense about him of undisciplined strength. He hurled the stick and the hound flew.

'What do they call you? Eh? How will you manage without a voice?' Only the unmarked side of his face showed, strangely still. The hound returned and they fought for the stick. Bayardine wrenched it from the shining mouth and hurled it again, right into the trees where it crashed and vanished. The hound's back rippled in flight.

'I could guess at it and you could shake your head. Can you shake your head? No? Well, I am not inclined to guess. What shall I call you?'

He sniffed, rubbing his nose, prancing about on the balls of his feet like a child playing ball, then turned around and faced the hut, shielding his eyes against the afternoon sun. Now the burned side ruled, all skinned and out of shape. The hound burst from the forest with the stick in its mouth and flung it at his feet. He turned again and was smooth.

'Burnet,' he said, 'that'll do,' stooped for the stick and raised it high.

Thank God I have a name. Burnet settled into his name with relief. Burnet. He tried a smile.

Bayardine laughed. 'What about my own?' he said. 'Very grand. French. What do you think came over my poor mother? A cottar's widow, you know. Shall I tell you what she called my brothers?' He threw the stick. 'And my sister? Tom. Jack. Margery.' With every name he struck the air. 'And Burnet. That's your name.' He laughed again, pushing away the hound that was leaping up like a mad thing.

'And me! Bay-adr-ine!' he declaimed, a fierce parti-coloured fool, then fell to the ground and sat, linking his arms loosely about his knees. His nails were bitten down to the quick. At once the hound fell to its belly beside him.

'She meant me for great things,' he said solemnly. 'Wouldn't you say?'

He is not much older than I am. I. Burnet. Burnet. But how old am I? He tried to think and the effort was like forcing his face under water. He closed his eyes. There was nothing in his head but a vague moiling darkness, full of thick cloud. There had been a picture, he remembered, it had come and gone, surely he could find it again. He pushed his mind through a mill. There. The hoof of an ox. Hard at its heels came another, altogether more distant, a child's fingers swiftly picking through a tray of seed. The hand was his own. He was small, sitting on stones, watching a black and white cat and a tall scrawny cockerel. The stones were whitened by the droppings of fowl.

'Your feet are bloody.'

He opened his eyes. His teeth were chattering.

'You must have shoes,' said Bayardine, rising. 'You will lodge with me. I wish it. Darby's dead. Up.' He held out his hand.

Burnet did not understand.

'Up!' said Bayardine, stooping to raise him.

The bloody bare feet walked slowly along a track through

flowering brambles, quite steady as long as he kept his eyes on them. Bayardine led him. They came to another clearing where young pigs grazed, a few hens pecked and thin garments hung drying on the bushes. Four or five huts clustered about and Bayardine led him to one. He stumbled down the step into the cool within and sat down upon a pallet bound with straw rope. Bayardine sat upon another and the brindle hound lay between.

'Darby's dead,' Bayardine repeated. 'He used to sleep there. See.' He pointed to where Burnet now sat, then dragged a basket out of the shadows and foraged in it, pulling out a very old pair of cordwain shoes that must once have been costly. 'These were his. Do they fit?'

Burnet put on the dead man's shoes. They fitted.

'Good! Good!' cried Bayardine. A sharp, eager look came upon him as he scrabbled in the basket a second time. 'I've got all these!' he said with open pride. 'Sometimes I wear them. And sometimes I let the others wear them. If I want to. I may let you. But they're mine.'

Then he drew forth his treasures, one by one, and laid them on the ground and across the pallets: fur collars and fine leather gloves, a gold ring, a silver comb, a tunic with a flowered border and a buckle fashioned like the head of a lion with gaping mouth. They shone in the gloom.

Burnet gaped.

'And this!' Bayardine stood, unfurling a scarlet cloak, the seams embroidered with periwinkles and turtle doves. With a flourish he threw it over his shoulders and strutted about with his head brushing the roof, two steps this way, two steps that, all the space the tiny hut afforded. 'Not stolen,' he said, preening. 'These are mine. *They* were stolen.' He pointed at the shoes. 'Darby pilfered them. But not these.'

He took off the lovely cloak and folded it away with the other things and pushed the basket away.

'Gifts,' he said, snickering softly, then sat and leaned forward, his one good eye steady and hard, the other violent under its meaty flap. 'Never touch them unless I'm here. Do you understand? No-one touches them unless I say. There's no need, see. What could you do with them? Nowhere fine to wear them. Can't run away with them. Nowhere to go! You never go back from here! Never go back!' He laughed and the ruined gums gleamed. Then he stood, suddenly brisk.

'Sleep,' he said, stooped to pass through the doorway and was gone.

Burnet lay down on dead Darby's pallet. Alone, his hurts returned. Never go back. Where?

He listened to the sounds of sawing wood and sighing branches, the moist snorting of a pig and the calling of birds. Some things he knew, though he did not know how. Someone had killed him and this place was death. But who had wanted him dead? Monstrous! He had harmed no-one. That he also knew. Tears of fear and self-pity welled in his eyes.

He looked down at the clothes he wore, searching for signs. They were not his own. But the breeches were and he felt in the pockets. In one he found a few crumbs of oatcake, in the other a small spiky thing wrapped in a dock leaf. How carefully he must have folded it away. Slowly, his fingers turned back the leaf.

It was a silver antler, skilfully crafted, tipped by a single ruby.

He stared at it for a long time, turning and turning it, passing it from hand to hand. So I too have a treasure, he thought. Pilfered? No. A gift.

He was sure of that.

olden-brown leaves had been raked and piled in drifts at the edges of the lawn where William and Sim crossed swords, circling like wary curs trying for a sniff. The contest lacked fire. It could have ended long since, but decorum forbade Sim from winning too easily, so they feinted and parried and mildly thrust, and the dull clashing of steel against the buckler on William's arm was like the endless closing of a door.

Sim smiled faintly. William, tight-lipped with unwilling concentration, found it in himself to hate that smile at times like this. His arm hurt and his nose ran and he wanted to go in and read by the fire with his favourite dog at his feet. The heavy sword spun from his stinging fingers once more and landed in the grass.

'I thought you had me then,' Sim said cheerfully.

William retrieved the sword. His hand put back his hair from his eyes, a habitual gesture. 'Devil with it,' he muttered. 'How much longer do we have to keep this up?'

Sim consulted the sky. 'One more try,' he said. 'We'll tell your father it threatened rain. Like enough it does. Trust me, the ladies will retire soon.'

William glanced ruefully towards his mother and his wife, sitting together on a bench on the terrace with their needlework. He felt graceless before them. Turning away, he sniffed loudly and wiped his nose. 'It will not rain,' he said gloomily.

'It will,' said Sim. 'Trust me. When am I wrong?'

'Oh, never,' sighed William, 'never, never, never,' and thrust at him almost with a will. A thousand nursery fights lay between them.

Sim laughed, rallying with an easy skill that sent William staggering. Sim felt spiteful. Why not? he thought. Why not thwack him, the great gawping dolt. Can't even get a word with him these days. If he sticks his nose up any more he'll fall over.

'A warsle!' he cried. 'A warsle!'

It was their old name for a wrestle.

Belle yawned again. She could not stop it.

'But then again,' May said sensibly, 'if it is a manifestation of Saturn, there is very little one can do. Until he has passed, that is, and the old devil is so *slow*.' Her eyes crinkled benevolently in the sun, peering down at the shining white silk of a shirt she was sewing very lovingly with tiny stitches.

'True,' said Belle. 'It will pass.'

They were discussing the fatigue which had afflicted her ever since the marriage.

'Of course it will. Is the sun in your eyes, my dear? No? I remember my mother used to make a brew of pimpernel and vervain—'

Belle let her hands fall idle on the seam she was embroidering, closing her eyes and letting the woman's voice wash comfortingly over her. In fifteen months she had grown fond of her mother-in-law. May never cast appraising eyes upon her waistline or nodded with hateful knowingness when she saw her eat a quince. She was big and stupid and peculiar, Belle thought, quite unrefined the way she laughed and scratched and probed her teeth like a bumpkin, quite silly the way she walked about grinning like a child. But she was very friendly and no-one else here was. Belle felt like crying again. She often did.

'You have no mother,' May had said. 'Call me Mother.'

And if May is my mother, Belle thought, then William is my brother, my poor little brother. I wish he was. Opening her eyes, she saw him turn laboriously, big feet blundering, thighs shaking in spite of the thinness of his legs. Poor idiot, she thought. He is very sweet. He didn't bother her too often, and when he did he was courteous. Things could be much worse, she thought. There was a chill in the air. On the lawn, steel clashed dully. His slim neck drooping, William walked to retrieve his sword. He was not distinguished in any way but sometimes when he was reading, occasionally pushing the lank fair hair back from his large bumpy brow, he had a certain elegance. She had noticed it from time to time.

Sim looked up and noted that she was watching and May was not. He mimed boredom, hand to yawning mouth, one leg hooked about the other, then straightened. In the interim between William picking up the sword and returning, he winked elaborately. The swordplay continued.

Belle smiled. She liked to watch the boys at play. Sim was always amusing and his freedom towards her no longer seemed strange, for she knew she was not singled out; even Harlock received such foolery. It was all but part of Sim's job now. Belle toyed with a blue silk, turning it this way and that playfully and watching the light change upon it. There was little enough diversion here. She stifled another yawn. The blue reminded her of the cornflowers that used to grow at the edge of the kitchen garden at Caddenhope, but the colour lost its resonance upon her uninspired seam, lying flat and dull with all the other weary strands. She was embroidering love knots and the thing would never be finished. When had she started it? She couldn't remember. She counted days, laid time away, there was so much of the stuff, it lay about her like a great sea lacking all wonder. No strange fish swam in it, no merman or maid would break the surface with a wild sleek head, no tempest call forth valleys and peaks.

She would sit here forever, sewing with her mother-in-law.

'Your nails are very white,' May said, smoothing the shirt over her knee with broad capable hands. For William, no doubt.

'I will have a cordial made up.' She continued smoothing and stroking as if the glistening silk were a pampered cat, till Belle thought it must wriggle and purr. May's hand appeared, covering her own.

'So cold,' said May. 'Our poor Belle. Look up, dear.'

Obeying, Belle saw the sky lightening over the trees that bordered the lawn. A leaf fell wearily.

May smiled. 'Now, melancholy,' she said, 'that is altogether a sterner fellow. There are potions.' She paused, looking sideways and deliberating, appearing to reach some conclusion before she continued. 'But I never knew one to work. There, you see. I have been troubled too. But that was many years ago and the season's changed.'

Her sensible powdery hand squeezed, smelling capable and a little perfumed, then she leaned forward and spoke inappropriately, in a vulgar, familiar way that she had, as if the two of them were young girls sharing a secret. 'There was a charm,' she said. 'Oh, if only I could remember! It was very simple and very beautiful, a certain cure for the melancholy.' She withdrew her hand and thumped herself on the thigh. 'I grasp at it, I grasp at it but it runs before!' All pale loose roundels, wimple and skin, she gazed over the tops of the trees to where the sun, lost behind clouds, made a shining white silk of the sky. 'Oh, the poor old woman,' she said. 'Her memory's gone. Gone completely.'

'Where did you learn all these charms?' asked Belle. This was not the first.

'Harmless things. My mother,' May said, pulling on a thread. She winked. 'Of course you know what they say about Herndale. Were you ever at Herndale, Belle?'

'Never. Though of course I remember all the trouble. I was very young —'

'I am so glad I was not living there at that time,' said May in a plain tone, taking up her work again. 'I was married by then,

you know. I said to my husband, that place is dead for me now.
I still maintain that it killed my mother.' She shuddered, shaking
her head and souring her mouth. 'I said I would never return
and I never did. One's childhood air, you see. I had such happy
memories of the place. I still do not wish to go back and think,
there, on that pretty spot where I used to play, that is where they
burned the woman, and there under the elm is where they
burned her daughter, and there stood that dear little house
where all the lads were set afire.'

Belle was a little shocked by this speech with its air of mild
vexation. She hated to hear of such things.

'Sim!' May cried. 'You are too close by far! Stand off, man!'

Sim skipped backwards. William took the opportunity to flick
back his hair and wipe his nose.

How terrible it must have been, Belle thought, to come here
as the bride of Harlock, to look out and know that home lay less
than a morning's ride away, just as I look out and think of
Caddenhope. And then, of course, she thought about John
Heron, and hated William and Sim on the lawn, and May's
voice going on and on about her girlhood and how she used to
see the woman going up and down the road with her basket, and
always some little scrub hanging about her skirts.

She crossed herself.

The wind blew the leaves over the lawn.

'I think the weather's turning,' Belle said.

A door clattered open behind them and Harlock's voice
echoed, giving orders to a servant in the house. His feet
crunched on the gravel, approaching.

'Say nothing of charms and suchlike,' May said swiftly. 'He
has no patience for such things.'

It was a needless instruction.

'I've had the damned toothache,' he said, striding before
them. 'Just a twinge. Most annoying.'

May raised her eyebrows. 'Strange,' she said, turning to Belle, 'this man has teeth like the eternal rocks.'

'Look at them,' Harlock said witheringly, sitting down heavily on a nearby bench and glowering at the pair on the lawn. 'What a pretty, pretty sight.' The smell of drink wafted from him, not unusual, and he panted, leaning forward with his knees widespread and his hands clamped on them. His head was low, swaying slightly like a bull about to charge. 'And what are you making, my dear?' he asked in a gruff tone. 'Something for your lily son?'

May did not hear.

'I've asked for a poultice,' he said.

He'll start to shout soon, Belle thought. Thank God he ignores me.

'What?' asked May. 'You know this is my bad side, please try and remember.'

'I've asked for a poultice!' he roared. Belle flinched. She hated the sweaty reek and grumbling breath, the slight sense of danger as if she were in the presence of an undisciplined mastiff. She imagined him in a muzzle and wanted to laugh. Hugh must be mad to like him, she thought. Flattered, no doubt, at the way he seeks him out. Looking up cautiously, she met Harlock's eyes and looked away quickly. They were misty from wine, full of challenge and unkind humour.

He sprang to his feet then, belched with great relish and paraded up and down before them, shouting fiercely across the lawn. 'Challenge him! Now! Oh, you great goose, William! You great fool!'

William faltered and Sim disarmed him. A bright red spot burned in William's cheek. May sighed. 'Sit down,' she said peremptorily. 'You block the light.'

Harlock stood still, his deliberate shadow in her lap. 'How much have I wasted on his tuition?' he said, blowing out his lips.

'Tell me that. Oh, wouldn't you love to see him in battle? Oh, wouldn't you?'

'He is not in that mould,' she replied, folding her work and turning to Belle. 'I think you are right, there's a chill in the air.'

Harlock laughed. 'Leaving?' he said, walking about again. 'So soon? I am amazed. Stay!' He spoke with a grin, pronouncing his words very deliberately and watching their faces. 'I am starved of the company of my kin, I find, and it is such company, such—well, what may I say?—such, such—the delights overwhelm me.' Turning on his heel at the edge of the terrace, he picked delicately at the small curls that decorated the ruddy criss-cross of his thick neck, staring at the lawn with the look of an irritated baby.

'What did he say?' May asked Belle.

'Nothing.'

'Higher! Higher, you fool! Oh, not *that* high! This is not a dance! You look like a prancing ape! God's teeth, I cannot bear it!'

'Have you done?' May asked him calmly. 'If so, please sit down.'

Harlock laughed again, throwing back his head and showing all his fine yellow teeth. 'Sim!' he called. 'Come here!'

Sim sheathed his sword and obeyed, lightly bounding up the grassy slope to the terrace and bowing perfunctorily in the direction of Belle and May. Alone on the wide expanse of the lawn, William stood looking this way and that awkwardly, unsure if he should wait or if the interruption meant freedom. We are alike in some ways, Belle thought, we are in the wrong soil. Weeds. Remembering the thin white blades of his shoulders when the moonlight filtered into her room, she pitied him.

'Bested you, did he?' said Harlock to Sim. 'Confounded you with his faultless skill as always?'

Sim spoke smoothly. 'Sir, we are evenly matched.'

'Liar,' said Harlock, rough and fond.

Sim nodded faintly, smiling at a space somewhere to the right of Harlock's shoulder. Old fool, he thought.

'Go to the stable, Sim,' said Harlock. 'Tell the boy I want the bay.' He looked at the sky. 'What do you say? Will it rain?'

'You know it will,' said May shortly. 'Where are you going?'

'To Caddenhope.' Belle looked up. 'Sim, you can ride with me.'

Sim nodded.

'A foolish way to treat toothache,' said May. 'Stay, Sim. You may take this to my room first.' She began gathering up her work.

'I'll risk the torment for a little good company,' muttered Harlock, watching William approach uncertainly across the lawn. 'I live in a nunnery. Isabel!'

Belle raised her brows.

'William's coming. Go and meet him. There, give your bits and pieces to my wife. Take him another way round. I do not feel inclined to look at his face.'

Belle stood up slowly, trying to put pride into the straightness of her back. 'Sir,' she said, 'will you greet my brother for me?'

'Oh, you need have no fear!' he replied expansively. 'I intend to invite him for a week or so of hunting before Martinmas. You will see your brother soon enough. Perhaps that'll put some life into your wheyface.'

She turned stiffly and walked along the terrace to meet William as he mounted the steps. She could not show her delight at the news, or her mortification at the petty insult that he threw away at her as if she were nothing at all.

'Oh, you are hateful!' snapped May, rising to her feet with the white silk trailing down.

He ignored her. 'Time she conceived,' he said, yawning and putting a hand on Sim's shoulder. 'How long is it now? A year or more and her belly's as empty as his head. Very poor stuff, oh, very poor stuff indeed! Sim could have done better.'

'Oh, you're a beast sometimes! Sim, take that smile off your face!'

Sim could not quite remove it, staring at the empty lawn as if it were a board on which some game were being played.

'You are both hateful!' she cried. 'You are forgetting yourself.'

'Why?' said Harlock, irritatingly amused. 'Why? Are not *you* forgetting yourself? Who are you speaking to?'

'To you!' she said, gathering up her work. 'Sim and Belle! It's horrible! She's your own son's wife!'

'And you are mine,' said Harlock nastily, 'and you'll have cause to know it if you don't guard your tongue.'

'Sim's a servant,' she said sulkily.

Harlock cursed softly, sweeping the air violently with one arm, then turned and marched away towards the house. 'Sim!' he called back, showing his flushed face over his shoulder, 'Come to my rooms shortly!'

May stood looking down, her nostrils all drawn in with pique. Sim turned his eyes on her slowly, no longer smiling. Oh, madam, he thought coldly, do you know how very much I dislike you? I know something about you. Shall I tell him, hey, hey, old sow with your big fat bubs? Shall I tell him you see a fortune-teller once a month? He'd beat you. Oh, don't you boke on *my* head, Madam. Think you're careful, don't you? Think no-one knows.

'Here,' she said, pushing the white silk and all her gear into his arms and hurrying after Harlock.

Sim stood like a statue on the terrace. 'Bitch,' he whispered, watching her go.

❖ ❖ ❖

'I am sick of the way you speak.' May strode into Harlock's rooms, where he stood adjusting his collar before a glass, his mouth a thin line.

He paused for a moment, then said, 'You are not very wise.'

She paced this way and that, hands folded at her breast. 'That's neither here nor there,' she said sharply. 'How long have we lived together as man and wife? Tell me that.'

'Tell *me*,' he said. 'My memory fades.'

'Twenty five years.' Stopping, she stared at his broad back. 'I don't expect you to be reasonable. I am just sick of it, sick of the way you speak to people, the way you speak about people, and in front of that slimy little toad. I'm beginning to hate the sight of him.'

He smiled. 'I spoke amiss?'

'You know you did!'

Sweeping a motley assortment of dogs from the great feather bed, he sat down upon it. 'I don't even know what you're talking about,' he said, bending to take off his shoes, 'I only ever speak in jest and you . . .'

'In jest! You insult your son—that is nothing new, you are always insulting your son—and now you are starting to insult *her,* and I am sick of it and I won't hear it.'

Harlock laughed. 'Oh, you won't! That is true. What indeed *do* you hear? And what, pray, do you intend to do?' He jumped up quickly, gratified to see that she stepped back. 'Do you see me tremble? Do you? Do you see me quaking in my boots? Ha! Or I would if I had my boots. Where are they? Ah, here they are. Now I will be well booted. We should all be well booted.' He burst out laughing, sitting once more to put on his boots.

'You are talking nonsense,' she said.

One by one the dogs crept back, nestling quietly against the cushions and on the bed-cover with its pattern of peacocks' tails obscured a little by grime and hairs.

Harlock stamped his feet on the floor. 'Truth is poor coin these days,' he said with grand, hurt disdain. 'Buys a man nothing but scorn. Brave soul that I am, I risk contempt to say what anyone with half an eye can see—that William is a poor excuse for a man. There! Why, damn me, I've said it again!'

'It is not as if you keep it in private,' she said. 'You insult me, you insult him, and now you insult his wife in front of that—'

'Oh, she'll shed no tears over it!' Harlock wet his finger and smoothed his hair carefully, curl by curl, and the more gently and nicely he did it, the angrier his tone became. 'What is she with her miserable face and her sicknesses, anyway? Indulgence! Homesick? Still in mourning? This is her home now and she'd better make do with it. Mourning? Fathers die. We all die. It's a wonder we don't have the old man's ghost wailing about the place.' And he laughed, 'I can see William mourning so for me! Ha, can you? *I* never behaved so unseemly when *my* father died, nor my mother. Would I? And do you see Hugh Rennock sulking or languishing on his bed of an afternoon complaining of an ache and putting out the servants? You do not. Well, hasn't *he* lost a father too? *You,* however, you took to your bed for a week when your mother died. As if it weren't the way of things.'

The more nervous of the dogs slunk off the bed and lay low amongst the folds of the curtains.

'Have you done?' she asked.

'Aye,' he muttered, his face heavy, and slung a mantle about his shoulders.

May stood for a moment then turned abruptly and walked to the door.

'I wish I'd had a son like Hugh Rennock,' Harlock said ruminantly. 'Or even Sim.'

'Sim!' she cried. 'Sim is a toad! That was a horrible thing you said.'

'What?'

'That,' she said. 'You know well what I mean.'

'I do not,' he cried. 'What are you babbling about, you silly woman?'

'That! About him and Belle! And while he was standing there with that idiot grin on his face!'

Harlock smiled. 'Why?' he said quietly. 'His blood's as good as yours.'

'That is not the point,' she said sourly.

'He's a good lad,' said Harlock defiantly, 'better than your own. Misfortune. That is all that lies between him and the likes of her. Come, we'll carry this no further, I must go.'

But May walked into the centre of the room and said to him heavily, putting a hand on his arm: 'That is the past and does not signify. This does. That he is a toad and she is your son's wife. Why do you make so much of him? He's poor company for William, always was, but you would never be told. They should never have played together!'

'His blood's as good as yours,' Harlock repeated. 'His family's history was not of his making,' and he added for good measure, to see her face: '*He* could have fathered a son on her by now, I'll be sworn. Unless she's barren. You were as bad, as I remember. Eight years of dead babes and then William!'

She stood quietly, remembering the swaddled things with their ancient wispy heads. The way her wimple sat made him angry. 'Water!' he said. 'I'm not surprised. Water comes of water. You certainly looked like an ale-wife, but you were always water between the sheets.'

She burst out laughing, rocking backwards onto the bed and collapsing by a small white hound that nosed her wimple playfully. 'You!' she roared. '*You* say *that!*' and she held her plump belly with one hand, pointing with the other.

Harlock advanced upon her with his hand raised.

'Clap me on the other ear! Do!' Laughter made her reckless.

He paused and ground his teeth against each other, rekindling the slight ache that had troubled him in the morning. Turning and sweeping from the room, he slammed the door so hard that it bounced open again. In the passage Sim stood with one knee bent and a foot on the wall. William hovered nearby.

'Sim!' Harlock cried. The white hound streaked by. Sim followed.

William hesitated for a moment then went and stood at his father's door, looking in at his mother, who sat upon the bed laughing so hard that tears filled her eyes. She stood up, wiping her face and sighing.

William took a couple of steps into the room. He hated disturbance. Sometimes he felt as if life was a mountain too steep to climb. 'Is it me, Mother?' he asked softly. 'Is it me you're fighting over?'

May ran to him and took him in her arms. 'No, my love,' she said. 'Not at all.'

fter midnight they left the dwellings and set off through the forest in the direction of Herndale, where Bayardine knew of a rich farmhouse that lay waiting to be plundered. Only the servants and the eldest son were at home, he said, and tonight the son slept with his mistress in the village and would not return before morning. There was a window, so high in the wall that no-one ever thought to secure it—he laughed, for it was known that he could climb like a lizard—giving onto a loft where the daughters slept, from which a stair ran down to the kitchen and the scullery, and a larder well stocked for winter. 'They ordered new leaded windows,' he said, 'but they've not come.'

Often Bayardine's knowledge seemed unearthly. Burnet had been awed at first, but was soon undeceived.

'Figs!' Dame Lane had said, crossing herself vigorously. 'He gets it all from his bawd! A filthy sinful creature, whoever she is. Aye! They'll have time to curse their foul lust when they're gnashing their teeth in hell!'

'Bayardine *has* no teeth,' said Edith, a thin girl who was in love with Rawl. And she'd wrinkled her nose. 'Agh! What woman could kiss that face?'

Some would, Burnet thought. What was left of Bayardine's face was strange and fell. He was wild and walked with a peacock swagger and his name was known. That would do for some, and indeed it did, in spite of the dreadful eye and rotten gums. Whenever Bayardine chose some finery from amongst his gifts, trimmed his beard and left for the world beyond to meet his sweetheart, Burnet would lie alone, envious and restless, touching one hand to the other, touching his face, touching and touching again and wondering whose touch he was reminded of.

It was said of Bayardine that he could see in the dark, scale any wall, enter any dwelling, cause sleep to fall upon servants and dogs. None of it was true. Bayardine was not brave but he was fearless and very skilled.

'Now I shall teach you how to be a ghost,' he'd said the first time they went thieving together. 'It is important for you to be a very good ghost. Eh, Burnet? Anyone may kill an outlaw, man's law won't punish and neither will God's, not in this world anyway. This is what we are taught. So be careful. Prepare the ground. Time's everything. Take an hour to open a door. Keep to the shadows, but if you must be in the light, think of yourself as some fearsome spirit and hope that's how they'll see you. You have no voice. Good! Less temptation to use it. Don't even clear your throat. And if you see someone, become a post.'

Burnet thought he was becoming a very good ghost now.

THIS one was very easy. The dogs were fat and lazy and the servants in the wrong beds. By dawn they were returning, he and I, the two best thieves, Burnet thought proudly, as they rested on a rocky plateau, and looked down upon the rook-infested tops of the trees in the last valley before home. Well before light they'd gained the frosty safety of the forest. In the sacks they had tallow candles and lye, salt meat and flour, oat-cakes, bread and barley, puddings and pies and some small fish tarts that had been left in the livery cupboard—all kitchen fare, for winter was coming and it would be hard. It was bitterly cold. Cocks crowed distantly and Bayardine crowed back.

'I can see their faces!' he said, laughing. 'The fairies are abroad! Spirits and goblins! Bayardine! Bayardine walks up walls!'

He strode about the flat rock with his hound dancing at his

heels. Behind him the sky was thick white. Here and there the forest was splashed with dark crimson. Many of the highest boughs were bare.

'Bayardine looks at steel and steel dissolves!'

The rooks flew up, shrieking. He cupped his hands about his mouth, tilting his head so that the hood fell back from his long yellow hair, made mad, piercing shrieks in answer and ran to the edge of the precipice, flapping his arms like wings.

'Bayardine flies!'

For a moment, Burnet expected him to step into the air; the ghost of a voice swelled impotently in his throat. But Bayardine turned, grinning his awful grin and wrapping his old cloak about himself. His breath hung before him. 'It is very cold,' he said. 'Jesus, it is cold. I am for my bed.'

He yawned like a dog, stretching every part of his mouth, then smiled at Burnet, watery-eyed.

'Brother Burnet,' he said fondly.

Bayardine had to have a companion. First there had been Darby, who'd had a liking for solitary outings and paid the price for it last winter. Now there was Burnet, who'd fashioned a notion of his predecessor as a man who spoke rarely and listened well, for Bayardine loved to talk, endlessly, night after night in the darkness of the hut they shared, each on his pallet with the fire dying down and the brindled hound scratching and sighing between them. The story was always the same. Bayardine, though young, trod the eternal circle that the very old travel, doomed to tell and retell, as if for the first time to a weary ear, the story of his life.

What could Burnet do but listen? He had no story to tell.

'They'll never get me. Never get Bayardine. I'm protected. Everyone dies but not Bayardine. Darby died. They hung him. He'd not have died if I'd been there. Fool.

'I wouldn't hang them. No, I'd put them in a fire, all the dogs of justice, and I'd build it wide around them and sit in a tree and watch them go up—whoosh! whoosh! spit! spit!—Where *you* bound, eh? Heaven or Hell? I don't care. I'll give you Hell now, I can do that. Oh yes, I can do very well for you! What am I? Death's Angel! Say it now! Who am I? Who am I? Death's very sweet and lovely Angel!

'Give me a pretty kiss, my pretty one. I am the fairest angel that ever there was and I'll give you a pretty little kiss. There. There.

'Such a sweet face.

'Listen, Burnet. Listen to this. One was Burnet, that's why I called you by this name. Burnet was the best. Tom and Jack were big brutes, used to push us down. *You* can't come, *you* can't come, scrubs.

'Yes I can. *I* can—not him but me. Oh yes, Bayardine was a rare thing even then. You can't stop me.

'Get away, our Margery says, you get away out of here, I'm sick of the sight of your face.

'I just stand there. Who says? Who says? Can't make me. *She* said. My mother, you see, ah, my mother, she said there was no-one like me. She'll make you do what I say, and she can, so you'd better leave me alone. Little beetle! I say. That's what you are, a little beetle running on the ground.

'Away! She throws the clout at my head.

'Har har, what good will it do you? If I have a bruise, you'll get a beating.

'All the sheaves of corn had to bow down to me. My mother told me that story. That's how it was. So they all had to serve me, and if they didn't I struck them with my fists and there was nothing for them to do about it. And strike them I did, all of them bigger than me—me being youngest, you see—and how they would mutter! Him! Little slug!

'Being blackbirds, wouldn't you think they could have

snapped me up with one peck? Would they dare? No!

'What do you think, Burnet? Was I a rascal? Well, they should have been soft with me. Poor Bayard! Poor little Bayard! Who'll play with poor Bayard?

'But then I got big, big as any of them, bigger, bigger, BIG-GER! Oh, I am the prince of them all, yes, I am. *Prince* Bayardine! Little Margery comes up to my armpits. Little Margery! She couldn't light a fire, you know, it never would catch for her. She hated me. She couldn't, couldn't light a fire. God, *God,* what they did to her! That night *I tore my face with my hands, tore my hands with my teeth, I would have torn them all to pieces if I'd got them!*

'And would still.

'And would still, Burnet.

'I've killed a few. Not enough. They'll not get me. Not Bayardine. No, not I, I am protected. Everyone dies, but not Bayardine. Darby died, you know. Stretched his neck a good deal, I heard. Be careful now, Burnet. All these things I tell you, all are for your good. Never forget.

'God, *God,* Bayardine calls on God. Do you laugh? I have talked to God. He didn't answer. I talked to the evil one too. Don't tremble! If he could do my work, who am I to complain? We're all damned here anyway, ask the priests. But he didn't answer either. Those two love silence.

'Silence!

'It occurs to me, Burnet, it occurs to me that you are very silent. Now, don't laugh. It occurs to me that you might be those two come to try me. Yes? Perhaps you listened with your double head. Did you? Do you whisper together after I have fallen asleep: What shall we do for poor Bayardine? What now? Softly! Don't wake him! Let us find a way to deliver his enemies into his hands.

'Whish! Whish! Whish! I can hear you! The wind in the trees!

'Poor Burnet. He thinks I am mad.

'Oh, I am growing drowsy!

'I am not mad. I am the one true soul in Christendom. They have all gone on before me. Listen! Listen to the wind! That was how it came. Like the wind,' —here his voice would drop— 'They are all abed but Margery and me. She's standing by the back door looking out with a flame in her hand, going to close the gate. You left it open, she says. There am I with one foot on the ladder, ready for my bed. Thirteen. A man.

'Strange the moment when you know. You *know*.

'Know what, Burnet? What did I know? Well, nothing, only that she went stiff. She was listening to something, and I saw that she was afraid and I went to stand with her—and then *I* was afraid too.

'I am never afraid now. Dead. Gone.

'But then I was, and it was coming off her like an ague. She knew before I did. It was like the wind in the trees, but there was no wind, no wind at all, it was a very still night, very starry. It gets louder. She's looking at me, the corners of her mouth are white. Looking at each other. Didn't know what it was but knew it was—what? What?

'Oh, I am sleepy! I want my bed, I want my bed!

'I never got my bed. It wasn't the wind, it was voices, a stinking mob coming up the road. It's your fault, she said. She could hardly speak. Your fault. Then she put the fire in my face.

'Well, I pissed myself. Ha ha! Bayardine, scourge of the land, pissed himself. Scourge of the land! I run away! I can't see! She runs for our mother. Here I am out in the copse with my face in the mud—Heard about it, did you?—Oh, there was great sport! The cat comes out on fire and dances all over the yard, runs up on our woodpile and makes a merry little blaze. The smell! My poor old mam, poor old mam! They've got her and Margery, they're taking them away. Thank God or the fiend, I cannot see. But I can smell it! And I can hear. The lads are inside, beating on the doors. They can't get out!

'Our house had good thick walls. Like a hundred killing days all come together, it was. The little pigs were all in there. Like your collops, do you, Burnet?

'They say my mother cursed them. She was watching. They shit themselves. Ha! The witch curses! Build the fire. Build two fires! Stop her mouth, stop the curses! She is talking to Satan!

'That was me. I talked to Satan. I lay with my face in the mud to cool it and it was melting, running away into the ground, and I talked to Satan.

'Well, you know the answer, don't you?

'Listen. Sh! The wind!

'And Margery, now, she couldn't even light a fire.

'Oh, I am sleepy! I am ready for my bed.'

They descended into the dense valley, fusty with decay, full of the chattering of small bright birds feeding on the holly berries and turning the leaf mould diligently. Slippery toadstools sprouted from rotten wood and the forest floor teemed with insects. But the air was fresh, full of the bite of growing winter, and Burnet felt his spirits rise as he neared home.

They passed through a bay of brown bracken, waist high, to the rank shore of a rocky little stream where alders grew, casting their shadow over the pool where in summer a great vat lay hidden for the cooling of victuals. Crossing on the flat stones where washing was pounded, they came to a great rock face, seamed and pitted to its distant height with channels of rich growth, and, after skirting its wild base for a while, turned in suddenly to pass under a veil of ivy and vanish. To a watching eye it might have appeared that they had entered the rock itself, but this was one alone of certain readily defended and invisible doorways into a massive bowl of a place, formed by the rock and a huge rambling bank of earth that had been made by men so long ago that the mind balked at it, for it must have been formed before the forest had grown up, and the land without the forest was unimaginable. The ramparts were shaggy now. It was possible to ride through the woods beyond and pass by and never know that the place inside existed.

They walked through the wood within, hearing voices at last and the sound of a bagpipe, and then the dwellings came in sight. The first chill of morning had gone and a few people were clustered about the central fire, where the smells of wood smoke and oatmeal gruel mingled. A pot bubbled and a dog scratched vigorously.

Burnet dropped his sack and went a little way past the fire, sat upon the ground and leaned his back against a heap of crumbling logs to watch as Bayardine showed off the spoils. Men and women and children came out of the huts and gathered round. Smoke drifted.

His tired eyes gave a dim, blurred quality to the scene before him, and the voices and the crackling of the fire were distant. He felt contented. Circumstance had bound him here with all these. All but the very young had lived before, in other lives before they'd left or been voided by the world to come their variable ways here. There were cooks and tinkers, sawyers and shepherds, beggars and thieves and fallen gentry, and the servants of great houses. Some carried scars that marked the passage from the old life to the new, mementos from stocks and gyves and pillories and stone vaults. A few lacked parts.

All of us died to come here, he thought. We are ghosts and the forest is our grave. When the cock crows we return to it. The thought pleased him. A kindly grave in spring, he thought wryly. Less so now.

A child ran past in the haze, trailing a long yellow rag of a thing. She fell and bawled. Someone picked her up and the rag lay dead in the dirt. Burnet pitied it. It was a weakness of his sometimes to repute lifeless matter with sense, so that he had on occasion found himself pitying kicked stones and crushed shells and rotten bean shucks, poor forgotten things abandoned as himself. He half rose to retrieve it but Edith walked by, stooped and picked it up, balling it casually in both hands. Rawl joined her and they stood together.

'Benjy found it,' she said, stretching the rag and letting it dangle. 'It's been beautiful once. Silk.' She put it round her neck.

'Filthy thing!' said Rawl, pulling it from her.

They fought for it, laughing and grunting, round and round till it fell at Burnet's feet, then dived for it together.

Burnet had it now.

'Mine!' cried Edith. 'I had it first!'

But Burnet would not play. He held it to his nose and sniffed carefully, cat-like. He did not know why. The wind and rain had washed it for so long that nothing remained, but something about the rag aroused him. Then, with a shock, he knew that he had seen this thing before, in the other life.

'Give it to me, Burnet!' said Edith, holding out her hand, but he snatched it away and rose, clumsy with haste, reeling a little as he took to his heels, never stopping till he had passed through the southern rampart and stood alone outside. The faint subsiding shudder of the ferns betrayed his passage. Great trees surrounded him, their stately presence wrapping him in silence and calming his breath.

He was so shaken that his knees were weak.

He went on till he came to a thin stony track that climbed steeply through holly and ilex to the flat side of a rock, from which sprang, as if by natural means, an ancient stone hut covered with ivy, the doorless entrance ragged, the ground before thick with toadstools and moss, trailing chickweed and bright herb Robert.

An anchoress had lived here many years before. No-one came to it now but the outlaws, who used a long dais of rock that jutted from the far wall as a resting place for their dead awaiting burial nearby. But Burnet sometimes came to sit and be still and search for memories, looking out of the open doorway and listening to the sounds of water dripping down the rock at his back, the wrens huddling for warmth in the ivy.

Crossing the threshold now, he sat down, sick with fatigue but unable to sleep. He'd found memories enough in this place, bright spangles strung upon a web, none of them connecting: a cat and a cockerel, a road through broom fields, fingers picking through a tray of seed; the neck of an ox, his own hands kneading it; an open doorway, dust floating in the sun-motes cutting through shade to a ladder; a cold, flat beach, small grey waves, the light of a lantern, the thin white arms of a woman.

Her arms, her face, her presence—she flitted from him sometimes when he woke, leaving him full of misery and desire. He could bear it all as a dream, but not this sudden clutch of real memory. He put the rag about his neck and knotted it over his scarred throat, fingering the frayed ends. How had it come here? It was not natural. It had crawled like a snake through the alien forest, torn and filthy, to tell him who he was, and he was afraid to hear. It would curl upwards, caress his cheek, whisper in his ear the story of his life. Don't you remember me, Burnet? Don't you remember?

Supper was over. In the hall the trestles had been cleared away, except for one, where Harlock sat with Hugh Rennock in the glow from the newly-banked fire, drinking wine and eating wafers and watching the exuberant tumbling of a woman with painted lips, who danced now upon her hands, now her feet, swaying and dipping lasciviously from one end of the hall to the other.

Ruddy, laughing men, replete after good sport and good food, sat along the benches and passed the ale around, and Harlock tapped his feet to the squeaking of a fiddle and thought how sad it was that life was not always like this. Hugh's company was a boon. The woman's limbs, revealed fleetingly and enticingly from time to time in the course of the dance, made him ache. He could have her, of course, but he would not. She was a crude, common creature.

He refilled the cups.

'What do you say, Hugh?' he said in a jocular tone. 'Shall we make merry each night you are here?'

'Indeed,' said Hugh, his eyes on the woman, 'nothing would please me more.'

The man was still so proper. Harlock drained his cup and poured again with the first nourishing draught still settling in his stomach, his senses jigging with the flailing bow and the leaping shadows.

'No ceremony, Hugh,' he said amiably, leaning forward across the board. 'After all, we are related now. Your sister is my daughter. My son your brother.' He laughed loudly and the laugh turned into a long clearing of the throat and he spat on the rushes. A pup inched forward and sniffed the slime, made as if to lick it but thought better and returned to the old rag of chicken skin it had been worrying.

'The claret!' Harlock cried. 'We must have the claret! Colour of honey—from Paradise, you would swear. Sim!'

Sim was there.

'The claret, Sim. Go to the . . . no, wait, we will leave it till tomorrow. Best it were savoured on a clean palate. Oh, a treat indeed!'

He waved his hand. Sim bowed and withdrew.

What is he saying? Hugh thought. I am his son? He has a son. He never drinks with his son. He calls him loon. He likes me.

The man is powerful.

Looking at Harlock's wide, glistening face, the strong hands cracking filberts, he found himself moved. For all the power, there was something of the child in the loose smile, the moist eyes following the dance. Harlock was very drunk again.

I must keep up, Hugh thought, taking a long, gulping drink that made him shiver in spite of the heat of the fire. What a soak, he's worse than me, and I'm a good drinking companion, a good man to have about, in the hunt and so on. Indispensable. Suppose I lived here, at Ellwin. I could keep an eye on her. And he looked about speculatively, catching the eye of a small silver unicorn upon a hanging, as cold and starlike as Belle's face since she'd left home. Caddenhope was a cold, empty place now, and he craved laughter, music, warmth, intoxication. Here, now, was a surfeit of all these things but they scarcely touched him. He had not drunk enough yet. That was it. Down it slid, down again, smooth as honey water. And this was not the best!

A roar from the assembly drew his eyes back to the dancer, who had turned somehow into a many-legged insect without a head. He flinched momentarily, unsettled by wine and weariness. Sleep was still no friend to him. But then he made out her knees and elbows, discerned her pudenda thrust towards him and the other cheering men, till she scuttled like a crab, sprang up and was whole again, walking ably on strong brown hands latticed with veins, her falling skirts exposing long legs that curled backwards like pincers. Then she was on her feet again, arms akimbo, smiling magnificently. Someone threw a roll and she caught it deftly, tossing it over her shoulder, before going to sit down by the wall, panting visibly and running her finger between her shoe and her foot.

Harlock was speaking.

'. . . a word in jest, that was all. And after all, the blood's the thing, not the rank. No harm done! She is too testy.'

Hugh agreed. He had no idea what Harlock was talking about.

'There, you see, you take no offence! And none intended! Your own sister, and you see the jest.'

'Belle?' said Hugh, puzzled.

'May is hasty.' Harlock banged the cup down, slopping a little wine. His words had begun to slur a little. 'Still, she is very fond of the girl, that is why. They are arm in arm.'

The fiddle launched into a new tune and the voices took it up, some bawdy catch that had everyone swaying and shouting and waving their cups about till ale splattered the floor. Hugh joined in. Some idiot danced like a bear till a kick in the rump sent him flying, and everyone roared. Hugh laughed, accepting more wine. And this seemed the truth and the rest a dream, and he thought he would spend the rest of his life drinking liquor with these good souls. He slid forward on the board.

Harlock called for a rousing song of battle. It ended on a cheer and he turned to Hugh with misty eyes that seemed happy and disappointed at the same time. 'When I was your age I could shoot well,' he said. 'I found a great beauty in that, Hugh.' He smiled. 'There is something very splendid in a flight of arrows falling together! I was fast. No sooner let fly one, the next is there! Good lads, good lads, shoulder to shoulder!' He laughed, with an air of slight embarrassment.

Hugh felt loose and twitchy. 'It is a skill like no other,' he agreed, standing and walking about before the fire with bold, jerky movements.

'Oh, there is a great pity in this,' Harlock said, 'a great pity!' and he shook his head, growing mawkish, 'to count the white hairs and dream of the fray. You cannot know that, you are young.'

'You are not so old,' Hugh said lightly, gesturing with his cup then drinking, striking a pose in the firelight the better to expose his youth and strength.

'I was a good soldier,' said Harlock, satisfied.

Hugh tilted the cup a little too far and spilled wine down his chest, overbalancing for a second and tottering. Quickly, he righted himself. The great hall whirled. He must sit down. He moved slowly, as if the air itself were some rich, restricting oil, and finding the bench, sank upon it. Shall I vomit? he thought.

'No more,' Harlock said simply, smiling fondly as he reached for his drink. 'The will is there but the strength no longer. Ah, the strength!' And he sighed.

He reveals himself to me, Hugh thought. The sound in the hall throbbed, near and far. Battle. Stink, blood, shouting, heat in the bowels. He raised his head, blinking rapidly and gulping air till he felt quite well again. Then he refilled both their cups.

'Your aim is faultless,' Harlock told him without rancour.

'That's true.' Hugh smiled. 'All I ask is that my skill match your reputation.'

Harlock laughed, leaning forward to clap Hugh firmly on the arm. His eyes were merry and pained, very moist.

The fiddle played sweetly now, sorrowing, out of tune with the hilarity of the men along the benches. Harlock blew his nose. 'Come,' he said briskly and drank. Wine glistened above his lip. He stood, raising his voice. 'Some life. What, is this a vault?' And he told a story about a woman who mated with a leper and gave birth to a monster. Laughter hung in the rafters. A song followed, about adultery, and some dolt capered down the hall with horns on his brow. Then came a song about a lady and a beggar, acted out with lewd movement and jeering mirth by two sweating brutes with eyes that rolled abominably.

Hugh took one drink too many and the sickness came back, rocking him. Leaning down to catch his breath, he noticed with that profound attention to the particular that extremes of drunkenness can bring, how the pup's attention had been captured by the movement of a single maggot that had emerged from under the rushes and was working its quick, undulous way across the space between two shadows. Cock-eared, the pup considered for a while, then snapped.

harlock stumbled on the threshold of his wife's room.

She turned, flushed and a little breathless, taking off her mantle. 'Confound the bird!' she said cheerfully before he could speak. 'Wouldn't come down from the cherry tree.'

'What?' He strode in, the breeze of his passing causing the candle flame to shrink and leap up again.

'Belle's parrot,' she said, dropping the mantle onto the red camaca of the bed. 'We thought we would have lost it.' Turning her back to him, she walked over to the high-backed chair, her affectation, which stood solitary near the window. Here she liked to sit and sew. She picked up the white shirt that had been laid by earlier, fondled it absently then dropped it again and went to stand by the window, where she lolled in an attitude of restless tiredness, stroking her hips absently.

'I thought it would rain,' she said.

She wore blue. Her thighs and belly bulged, pronounced by her stance. Harlock went over and stood behind her, full of heat, putting his arms about her and pressing close to nibble the side of her throat and the rim of her ear. He felt the slight involuntary shrinking of her muscles. Tight, hard, short of breath, he glued himself still closer with a quick, sharp movement.

'Oh, mercy,' she said, 'you stink.'

He reached for anger but could only raise a vague sadness. Lust always weakened him. 'Ah, come on, May,' he murmured, 'there, love,' stepping round in front of her and trying to kiss her lips.

She pushed at him with mild annoyance, unconcealed. 'Come on, then,' she said as if to an importunate child, 'only you

❖ 89

must turn your face away. Your breath's enough to make the Devil boke.'

He chuckled, hopefully stroking her sides and rubbing the whole weight of his body into her back and buttocks as they moved to the bed.

'Wait,' she said, irritated, and sat down and started fiddling with her veils, but he pushed her back upon the cushions impatiently and began pulling at her skirts, wiping his beatific face against her bosom. With a sigh that was scarcely perceptible, she turned her face away, holding her breath and helping him find his way through the tangle he was making of her clothes; but when it hit home the poor blind worm could only butt vainly, bruising its head and growing flabbier with every heave, till he groaned in fury and flung himself off her with a curse.

'No matter,' she said quietly.

He looked at her with wounded eyes.

'Now, go to bed,' she said, rearranging her clothes, 'and sleep it off.'

He saw that she was relieved.

Without a word he left her, hardening as he strode back to his own apartment. His jaws moved. 'Sim!' he roared, striking a sleeping cat from his pillow and scattering cushions. 'Sim!'

He flung himself down.

Sim appeared in the doorway, calm.

'Bring me fresh water, I'm parched.' He tossed his head, searching his mouth for moisture. 'Quick!'

Sim withdrew.

Harlock, alone, gave way to temper, arched his body and beat his fists at his sides, gritted his teeth, jumped up too quickly and staggered as he pulled down from the wall a long keen sword. 'Hah!' he cried, 'Hah! Hah!' wielding it this way and that, thrusting, driving, whirling to decapitate an imaginary enemy. Sim entered and set the water jug down, bowed and left without a sound. Hurling the sword aside, Harlock fell upon the jug and gulped, the water spilling out of the sides of his mouth and hanging in small silver droplets in his beard. It was icy cold and set his bad tooth throbbing.

Belle watched from the window as the starlings came in to roost for the night, each stippled swarm approaching as a single body, now a serpent, now a cloud, vanishing, billowing, crossing the thick sky to the forest's edge. From time to time a great roaring of wings rose aloft from the trees, subsiding as more arrived.

She became aware of the silence a mere second before she spotted the hawk in a nearby thicket. The forest seemed to hold its breath, and a new flock came straggling home. The hawk rose swiftly on heavily beating wings, jesses trailing from its feet, was into it before a single bird could know, and a terrible clamour began, the flock splitting and tearing like frayed silk. The hawk took a bird on the wing and carried it away.

The parrot in its cage ran this way and that on the perch.

'Sh,' she said, 'sh, my pretty pretty, no-one's hurting you,' and went on watching till it was dark, when Sim brought her a new candle.

'You look tired, Sim,' she said as he bent to light the wick, humming under his breath.

He shrugged, stifling a yawn and adopting a pose of extreme lethargy as he rose. 'On the contrary,' he said, 'I have nothing to do but nursemaid's tasks this evening. So here I am humming some old nonsense such as my old nurse used to sing.' But then he folded his arms and smiled at her frankly. 'Yes, I am tired,' he said.

She smiled back. His company was always pleasant, and she loved his history, so diverting, so full of shadows and dire consequence: there was a father beheaded for giving succour to the

King's enemies, a mother disgraced by self murder, sisters sent to swell the ranks of the Benedictines. Stirring tales, she thought. Perhaps they accounted for his manner, which could be unctuous and insolent all at once.

'I've taken water to my lord, fruit to yours, wine to your brother . . .' he numbered them on his fingers, hesitating briefly and adding with a faint touch of mischief, 'and I'm about to take a sweet cake to my mistress. She always has a sweet cake before she retires, that's why she resembles the white mare.'

He watched her without blinking, unsure yet inviting complicity.

Belle's smile faded. 'The white mare?' she echoed faintly.

Perceiving his mistake, he blinked once and wiped the tip of his nose with a movement both clumsy and arrogant. 'The fat one,' he said defiantly.

Belle regarded him thoughtfully for some time. He looked back, stiff and still, and rain began softly. The moment became uncomfortable.

'Sometimes you go too far,' she said.

He nodded. 'Pardon, lady.'

She softened. 'Oh, pardon granted,' she said.

He left her then, standing for a moment in the passage to make foolish faces at the wall. 'Sometimes,' he whispered, 'you go too far,' and sauntered over to a great basket that sat beneath the window at the end of the passage. It was half full of dirty linen, which he removed. Coming back past her door, he paused. She was talking to herself.

Drawing close, he put his ear to the door.

The words had ended and the sound of muted weeping was low. He withdrew, hesitated, returned and made as if to knock, then walked quickly away.

THE sharp tang of rain came in at the window. Belle walked about the room, endlessly. She jumped onto the bed and pounded her head upon the cushions. This must be how mad people go, she thought, sitting up and gazing about distractedly, feeling an urge against all reason to run downstairs and out into the wet night, for nothing more than to be outside these cold walls. She hated this place. She'd lost count of the hours she'd spent in this room looking out towards the forest, talking to herself, talking to the bird in its cage, crying for home and father and brother, and for John Heron—she thought of him now as she listened to the rising wind blow rain against the thick walls. Whenever she thought of him, he was on a road somewhere, always walking and never arriving. He was cold, soaked to the skin, his hair dripping, and he was in need of a good cloak.

She lay down and kissed her pillow, sliding her arms around it softly and holding it close. 'Oh, sweet heart,' she crooned, 'my sweet heart,' nibbling its seam. Then with a sigh she rolled onto her back and gazed solemnly at the canopy overhead. Everyone talked of the possibility of an uprising. Keep him away from thieves and rebels, she thought. Let him keep to the side. She sat up, cold, suddenly afraid. Those who talked about blood couldn't know, could they? The people in the fields and the women drawing water and all those little weathered children, John Heron himself, the whole rout of them—she saw them storming the gates, raging through the hall with clubs and pikes and axes, mashing and splitting and slitting.

Me? she thought. Will they kill me? No, no, no, not me, not me.

Then she imagined riding out one day and seeing a man slowly turning on a gibbet, and the face coming inexorably round, bloody holes where the crows had plucked, was John Heron's.

Someone knocked on the door. William, she thought wearily, rising slowly, brushing herself down and going to let him in. But it was Hugh, standing in the shadows. 'Alms!' he cried, 'alms!' and came in laughing.

'Fool!' she said, kissing him, then stood back to scold him lightly. 'I don't see the point in you coming to stay,' she said. 'You spend all your time guzzling with that odious old man.'

'Odious? Harlock? Belle, he is an innocent babe, you do not know him.' He went to make mouths at the parrot, which was preening itself and preparing for sleep, an expression of idiotic benignity on its face. He's drunk again, she thought. 'I wish I could come home,' she said.

'I wish you could,' he said.

The place seemed strange. They remembered their child-hoods. They embraced for a moment, then withdrew from each other. 'Well,' she said, 'how strange that I should not be able to think of a thing to say to you. We used to chatter. Didn't we?'

'We did. I have no-one to talk to now. Listen, I should marry. What do you think, Belle?'

'Of course you should.'

'The old house is a vault,' he said, speaking with drunk deliberation. 'You must come and see it. It is your home, you will find it very sad. Ellwin, now, I see, is not your home. What a cold, rambling place this is! It quite chills me—' He looked about morosely.

'It's never warm,' she said. 'Well, *you* have changed.'

'Are you never afraid of it?'

'Of what?'

'The house,' he said.

'I'm not afraid of it.' She snorted. 'I hate it, that's all. You're still a baby, Hugh. Just the same. There's nothing here but walls and stairs.'

'Well, I've come to tell you,' he said, swaying towards her with a bleary look, 'I've come to tell you what I hear now in that old house, and if you aren't made scared by it . . .' A door far off closed quietly and he started.

'Hugh!' she said. 'Stop this! When do I see you? Hardly at all, and when you do come, you spend all your time with Har-lock and only come to me like this, all starting and trembling . . .'

He laughed, but his eyes unsettled her. 'Have done,' she said.

'Some day I'll tell you what I hear,' he said. 'In that house. On the stairs.'

'Have done. You can't frighten me.'

He went to the window and looked out. He hated the nights. Sometimes the stairs creaked and he thought of his father and John Heron. He'd never spoken to John Heron before the day they went hunting together, but he missed him now from the fields with an indulgent, almost fatherly regret. Sometimes he dreamed he walked laughing with John Heron in bright sun-light, and when he woke, the cold sweat of nightmare was drying on him.

'It's only the dark,' she said, coming up behind him.

Only the dark. What she always said, coming to his room when the nightmare roused him. Hugh, it's only the dark.

Hugh cleared his throat. 'Say what you used to say.'

'What?'

'What you used—what you used to say.'

'I don't know what you mean,' she said patiently.

'Morning soon. You used to say, Morning soon.'

She laughed. 'Did I?'

Well. Morning always came in the end.

Sim had been despatched to find a young spaniel that had strayed. He disliked dogs. When he found it trying to dig a way into the hen run he gave it a quick dig in the flank with his toe before handing it over to a kennel boy. The thing squealed like a stuck pig, and Sim smiled with weary malevolence, wishing it were William. Has time for dogs, he thought dryly. Time, Sim, has the better of me, the great soft thing says. Time enough to wear his eyes out over a book. Time, indeed. Yes, sir, yes, sir, at once, my dear sir!

It was a pleasant morning. After the rain the scent of the earth rose, and a dove murmured. Sim saw William and Belle come walking up the sanded path that ran between the rose garden and the herb garden, and his smile increased. A wonderful neck she had. Poor little maid, weeping in her room. William spoke and then she spoke, smiling. What could they talk about? William was a gentle, silly soul. She could not like him.

He found himself moving to meet them, his devil rising. Make him a fool in front of her, do, make him a fool. And he is, he is. This devil of mine, he thought. Down! Down!

He met them on the terrace. She was turning her head aside and smiling and the way her hair was dressed made her neck look snappable. Sim bowed in exaggerated style, a prelude to some witty remark still forming, but before he could speak she relinquished William's hand and swept inside with only a faint acknowledgement, not even meeting his eyes.

Straightening, Sim looked at William.

'Well?' he said, familiar.

'Well?' said William.

Neither knew what to say. They never spoke these days.

'Did you find the pup?' asked William.

'Decimating the hens,' Sim replied. 'I sent a boy to the kennels.'

'Oh. Well. Have it brought to my room.' William smiled, starting to walk away.

Sim had a sudden urge to seize his retreating collar and yank him back savagely, turn him round and strike him in the face. Instead, he ducked around to the front and hit him lightly on the shoulder, grinning. William looked surprised.

'A warsle,' said Sim.

William moaned. 'I have my good hose on,' he said.

'No matter.' Sim squared up brightly. 'You have more.'

William stood uncertainly. He was always unsure of Sim now. Everything had been simple once. He didn't think Sim was supposed to speak to him like that. Then, unprepared, he stumbled backwards as Sim tackled him. This was unfair, Sim had always been stronger, always. William felt ridiculous.

'I said no!' he cried, but Sim went on as if he had not spoken.

William's rare temper erupted and he lashed out furiously, catching Sim a blow in the ribs that amazed them both. He stood back at once and smiled, pleased with himself.

'Oho! What's this?' was all that Sim said, catching his breath.

They stood panting, tense, and before anything else could happen William's nose began to bleed profusely all down the front of him, splashing the grey silk of his doublet and his best brown hose. Stunned, they looked at the blood. William touched his nose and looked down at his bright fingertips. Then they began to laugh.

'What are you doing?'

May's voice cut in. She was holding the door open, leaning out by the hollyhocks.

'I had a nosebleed,' said William, and the two smothered laughter.

'What?'

'He had a nosebleed!' Sim shouted.

'Don't shout!' she cried, wrinkling her nose in annoyance. This forward little churl with his ugly pig nose! She had been arguing with her husband about the kitchen finances and her head ached. I must lie down, I must lie down, she was thinking. Why is William covered in blood? 'Go and bathe it at once,' she said.

William looked as if he might speak but did not, glancing once as he left at Sim, and it was so like their old childhood fights that both of them laughed again. Alone with her, Sim's devil rose, thumbing its nose. He went on laughing, too familiar, too long and loud, too insultingly, staring merrily straight into her eyes, an indrawn smothered snort of a laugh that seemed to emerge from the space between his nose and mouth.

She just looked at him.

He laughed on, putting all that he could of insolence into it, afraid suddenly that he had gone too far. But he was damned if he'd stop. Not for her.

'Stop that noise,' she said.

How greatly I dislike you, madam. How very greatly. And you'd better be careful how you tread with me, you stupid woman, I am warning you. He did not speak but she saw something in his eyes. She took several heavy steps towards him, leaning forward and striking him once, hard, across the skull. Too hard, she thought at once. 'Who do you think you are?' she said, regretting it all as she said it, 'You are replaceable,' then turned abruptly and walked away.

Oh, I am replaceable now. Thank you.

Go to the kennels. Get the dog for William. (Wring the thing's neck.) Oh, but I know where you're going. I know where you're going, yes, I do. *You* have no power, for all that you speak to me like a dog. Now. Go to the kennels.

But he stood for a while, his ears burning and a sinking feeling inside him. His eyes clouded over and his throat filled, but only for a second or two before he put on his customary face, with the smile.

He felt the sting of her hand. I'm going to tell tales on you, he thought. He'll beat you. Oh yes, he will, and then I'll get to watch.

He had the dog delivered to William. After dinner, Harlock called for him, wanting him to play a game of chess to wile away

the afternoon. It was the perfect opportunity. Harlock was liver-
ish, his eyes deeply sunk. He'd drunk too much with Hugh
Rennock the night before, and his tooth had begun to trouble
him. 'I'll have to have it pulled, I know,' he grumbled, poring
over the board.

Sim did not speak. He'd been carefully unlike himself since
he'd entered the room. The rain began again and he looked
towards it pensively.

'What's the matter with you?' Harlock asked testily.

Sim did not speak.

'For the love of Christ!' Harlock sat back from the board.
'Where's the sense in this? If you're ill, go and lie down.'

'What would I do,' asked Sim, not looking at him, 'if I knew
something I was not meant to know, and it concerned you, yet
to tell you would be'—he raised his shoulders—'would be—'

'What are you talking about?' Harlock snapped. He hated
being made to feel stupid.

'It is not an easy thing,' said Sim, hanging over the board, his
chin in his hand. There was a silence.

'An easy thing?' Harlock snorted his exasperation. 'What are
you talking about? Oh, I'm not having this! Come on, now, if
you have anything to say that concerns me, say it. Then I'll tell
you whether you should have told.'

'Well,' said Sim, 'it's only that I know your dislike of fortune-
tellers—seers—all that crew.'

Harlock did not prompt him, so he continued. 'There's this
woman lives near the beck, procures abortions, reads palms,
gives simples and so on. It's my mistress. She goes there sometimes and I am worried for her.'

Harlock's face did not alter. 'Go on,' he said after a while.

Sim looked away. 'That is all,' he said.

'How do you know about this?' asked Harlock.

I'm clever, you fool, thought Sim. Isn't it obvious? I notice things. 'I go fishing,' he said, 'in the beck. I have seen her go in.'

Harlock leaned back and was still for a long time, chewing a nail. 'Confound this tooth!' he said thoughtfully.

Sim sat back too, watching him. Beat her. Beat her for it. In her room. I can watch through that crack in the door.

'How many times?' asked Harlock.

Sim considered. 'I have seen her go in three times,' he said. 'She stays for quite some time. But I have noticed something else.' He pursed his lips, drawing breath in through his nose and pausing for effect. Come, Sim, his devil said, don't overdo it. 'Sometimes, you know, she takes a morning walk as far as the bridge?'

'Yes,' said Harlock.

'She has a little horn that she takes with her. Do you know the one? It hangs by the door in her room—'

'Yes, yes,' said Harlock. 'It belonged to her mother.'

'She sends a message. If she blows an *appel de gens* to the west, she will ride over in the afternoon. It never fails.'

'What do you mean?' Harlock looked more puzzled than angry. 'What are you telling me?'

'That is all I know,' said Sim.

Harlock went over to the window and looked out at the rain. It was getting wild out there now, the moisture dancing in front of his eyes. 'Why would she do that?' he asked gruffly, with an embarrassed air. 'Why blow the horn?'

Sim shrugged faintly. 'Well,' he said, 'I know very little of what goes on at these—meetings?'

'Meetings?' Harlock turned sharply. 'What meetings? Are you saying that other people are there? Are you saying that my wife takes part in . . .'

'Oh, no, no!' said Sim quickly, beginning to regret a little what he had started. Visions of unholy sabbats unwound in the room. For all he knew, the silly woman just went there for a face

cream. 'I have never seen anyone else. No, I only meant, perhaps, well, how would I know, but perhaps there are prepara-
tions to be made—potions, perhaps—perhaps she sends word
that—'

'Potions!' Harlock was furious now. Sim felt a little chill of
power. He would beat her now, surely. And all because of me,
he thought.

Harlock was silent for a long time, thinking hard. I have told
her, I have told her. Could the woman not keep her secrets
better than that? He felt tired, unfit for the match. The woman
had a filthy tongue, and there'd be war for weeks. The thought
made him angry and he came over to the chess board and beat
it so hard that the pieces jumped and rolled. Sim righted them
meticulously, as if there were any chance of this game ever being
finished. He saved the best till last.

'Sir,' he said, 'she is going there today.'

There would be fun now. His blood stirred.

harlock rode briskly among rambling copses and rising hills that billowed about him like a buoyant sea. As he rode he sang snatches of song, trying to raise a heartiness that he did not feel. It would be good to live at peace for a while. These petty domestic brawls irked him, as his tooth was beginning to again, damn it, but what could he do? Damn Sim! Boy enjoyed telling me, he thought with a touch of disappointment.

He had given his wife a start of twenty minutes or so. She would be well settled as he arrived and he would walk in and frighten them to death. The old hag, whoever she was, would remember the burnings and piss herself. And May—who did she think she was? Talking to him as if he were anyone, looking at him as if he were a basket of laundry. He should have beaten her ages ago.

Let her disobey him this time, he thought, and pricked the horse on tetchily. The cold air made sharp, dancing jabs of pain deep in his jaw and he thought about being home in the warm, holding a hot cloth to his face.

Over the next rise a low farm cottage came in sight, with a yard, a field for a cow, and a stubble bank sloping down towards Ellwin Beck, which roared along over its glassy green rocks a short distance away. May's horse was in the field. Harlock began to ride down, keeping to the trees, but reined in when he saw a movement on the side of the wide gully through which the beck cut.

A growing mizzle made the air fine and filmy and grey. He narrowed his eyes to see. It was a tall man, heavy-set, with a hood concealing his face and a thick cloak about him. Harlock could see only the side of him. He had a quick, light tread, and came down swiftly through the ferns with a big dog at his heels. On a small plain of couch grass where the beck pooled, the man paused to look at his reflection in the water, out of sight of the house. Then he moved on, stepping on the stones and crossing an outcrop of rock that was beginning to shine, till he stood at the top of a rough incline above the house. He loped the last few yards with a sureness on that craggy ground that must have come from long familiarity.

His dog ran wide after something and he turned his head for a second. The sound of his voice calling it to heel was a blur, like the weather. The face was a purple shock.

Harlock felt as if he'd seen a ghost or some storied monster.

The man was at the back door of the farmhouse. Before he could knock, it was opened and Harlock saw May reach out and draw the man in, pulling him into an embrace and raising her face to his before the door was even closed.

The leaves began to drip. This was a foul spot, damp and dark with the land rising all round, full of waterfalls. May had just kissed the local demon. Bayardine.

Impossible. Bayardine burned with the rest. All this talk, all these mumblings—people loved stories. Harlock felt sick. Impossible. That was her. May? In that house with Bayardine. His tooth raged. I am too ill for this, he thought. Bayardine is dead. He is alive. May kissed him. She kissed that face, she must be mad. How old is she? Am *I* mad? She is old, she would not—

But then, he thought, how hideous the man is. What young one would have him?

Dogs roamed the yard. He must go down, find the truth of this. Bayardine is mad, he thought, a savage. And I am ill. He drew back into the trees, watching the house.

Would anyone else want her?

She's a cold woman. But *that* was not cold, just now, the way she drew him to her.

Ravens flapped lazily on the far side of the valley, one, two, three. Oh, curse it all, he wanted to cry, why could not things stay as they were? Why could they not leave him in peace? Now he would have to ride down there and—

What? Bayardine is a young man. Strong. They all say he is strong. Like a beast. Hates mankind, they say. He might kill me. She kissed him. What would she do, would she stand and watch? No! It is impossible. He thought of the folds of her skin, soft and large, shook the thought away and looked down. That great brute of a dog down there. No chance of an unheralded approach. Lies. Deception. Oh, very grand she is when I make a small jest, and here she is stealing out and keeping trysts with the dregs of the land in some foul, miserable place—

The house must be razed.

FOR an hour he sat cold on his horse, spurring her up and down a little through the trees for warmth now and then, never quite losing sight of the house. An hour. The ache in his tooth had spread all over his head till he felt like tearing it from his body. An hour. More. What is she doing? Why is it all so quiet? A cold rage, pent and terrible, grew within him.

Whenever he blinked he felt the soft moisture the mist was depositing on his eyelashes.

I know what she is doing! he thought. I know what she is doing! God, damn this pain!

And then the front door opened and a boy emerged and fetched May's horse. She came out alone and mounted in the yard and set off smartly along the homeward track. She must pass this way. He drew deeper into the trees, hating himself for doing so. He'd meet her in the way and have it out with her. He would slap her face. Slap her hard. She must ride along behind him, weeping. The thought revived him a little and he moved his muscles, dispersing the cold.

The figure of Bayardine emerged from the back door and set off the way he had come, towards the place where the beck pooled. Oh, but wait, thought Harlock, I have caught Bayardine. I have him. Christ! What a trophy. Bayardine walked confidently, a youthful, easy vigour in the movements of his limbs. Harlock held his breath. Let her pass. Let her pass. Bayardine had a new cloak. With a slight thrill, he recognised it as a good, hardy one he himself had worn a great deal a few years ago.

He heard the approach of a horse and hid.

May looked like a woman returning from market, pleased with something she had bought. She wore make-up, he noted, a hectic spot on either cheek that made her look older than she was.

She passed, unaware of him.

After a while, he followed. Let him think, let him think. Soon he would know what to do.

He ate supper alone and did not attend the evening mass, but lay back upon his bed with the curtains drawn and a poultice on his gum, listening to the bells. The pain was less but he was exhausted and felt very old. He must sleep well tonight, that's what was needed. He rubbed his eyes.

There are those that like them old. And she is rich. She is not unhandsome. Does she give him my money? What a fool she has become.

How have they met?

It is possible, it is entirely possible. She was always a fool for charms and soothsayers. Such places where they'd be attract dirty company like shit attracts flies. How could the woman be such a fool? What? Does she think she has anything a man like that might want? What does he want? Like a mare and a wolf.

Impossible. He saw it, a wolf covering a mare. He winced. He might kill her. Savage teeth. Beast. Alive, no doubt, with pox and worms and worse.

People know about this! How many? The old hag, the boy who fetched the horse—who beside, who beside? How many of the smirking idiots laughed behind his back when he rode by on the big bay horse? How many capered after, drooling and squinting and horning their brows. Might as well ride backwards and have them throw filth.

Does he boast to the scum of the forest how he dings the great lord's wife, how she fawns on him, how she tells him with a laugh—his blood ran cold—that Harlock's great stinkhorn dwindles into a puffball on contact with her unyielding flesh?

Laughter rang in the forest.

Soon there would be true winter hunting, with snow in the forest and spoor everywhere. They would hunt roe. His eyes burned. She had spoiled it all for him. All the pleasures were tainted. Harlock squeezed his eyes and drew back his lips and a dry cry came out.

Sim came to the door. The little brute was afraid. He set out a night light and a chamberpot, scarcely speaking. He is wondering, Harlock thought, he sees me changed. Doesn't know what his tattling brought on. I'll not tell him. Let him wonder.

'Do you want anything else, my lord?' Sim asked quietly. His face questioned further. Harlock shook his head and dismissed him, then lay down. The moon was nearly full.

It was a long night.

She chose such filth. Had he not smelt it on her? He shivered. She has batted me aside like a fly. So proud and all the time rutting with a beast.

What could he do? He could do anything.

He saw Bayardine with his terrible face stealing into this house at night, walking through its passages with that same familiar step with which he'd come down from the forest. The man was a grub in his brain. He could not bear to think further. This image remained, growing sharper.

At first cock his tooth began to twinge again. He opened and closed his eyes on grey candle light. I should kill her, he thought. Anyone would. I should run her through. What would she look like, dying? He shuddered. Damn it all, he needed sleep.

None came. Harlock's body felt tired and old.

He saw himself in single combat with Bayardine, and Bayardine won. It was the dead time of night. Vengeance is mine, he thought, that should be true, then fell into a purgatorial sleep, dreaming that he unmade a hart, skilfully removing the most tender morsels and spiking them on the *fourchée*. The slippery innards were like a wet mouth eating his knife. A long tongue flapped upon the *fourchée*. He held up the testicles on his silver fork.

Harlock cried out in his sleep.

Towards dawn he woke and lay watching the sky at the window, waiting for it to lighten. He must act immediately. What he did must be quick and thorough and end this thing once and for all. He would not kill her, no, but she must see what she had done. Then he would send her away.

She would always know that she was obliged to him for her life.

He fell asleep again, waking afraid, but it was only Sim coming in with a light and some wine. He drank some and felt better. Sim pulled out the cloth and fetched warm water.

'Three things, Sim,' said Harlock, dressing.

Sim poured water.

'First, another poultice.'

Sim nodded.

'Then go to Hugh Rennock and tell him I want to speak with him after mass.'

Sim held out the bowl and Harlock dabbled in it.

'Then,' he said, 'go to your mistress's room while she is at breakfast, take the small hunting horn that belonged to her mother, go as far as the bridge and blow an *appel de gens* to the west as you have seen her do. Put the horn back. Do not speak of this to anyone. Do exactly as I say or I will have you beaten. Do you understand?'

Sim's face did not alter. Me? Beat me? He began to comb his master's hair. He could not fathom this new game and his unease grew.

When he left, Harlock stood quite still for a while. A sense of the ridiculous assailed him. Of course, the man would not come. Why should he? Why should he hear it? Or why should he not suspect a snare? After all, he'd seen her only yesterday. What would he think? The old woman craves it. He would turn to his comrades, the ragged, fetid crew, and they would laugh obscenely.

There must be no possibility of failure. Injured, any wild beast was deadly. Hugh Rennock was skilled with a bow. Kill me an outlaw, he would say—privily, you understand, we want no judge and jurors, that would take too long—and I will give you the good bottom land just north of Caddenhope.

He'd do it, Rennock would. For that, for friendship, and for the dignity of killing Bayardine.

ho was she? Above her right shoulder could be seen a conical mountain with a spiralling yellow road rising through flowery meadows. She had given him the antler, he was sure of it, yet he saw her as if framed in a picture.

He did not know where it came from. It was not real life.

Burnet turned over in the hut and fell into another sleep. He slept often now these dark times were here. Sometimes the sky stayed low for days on end, obscuring the tree tops, and then the forest lived in perpetual twilight.

Burnet sucked his thumb as he slept. When he woke he was hungry. He was hungry all the time, though he never starved. He lay watching the thin red glow of the fire in the hut, never blinking till his eyeballs burned, thinking of the life he had inherited. This place grew wilder with the coming of winter, the people more unkempt, the children lean and fast with birdlike eyes. The rain put out the central fire, and Dame Lane walked about soaked, grimacing like a fiend. The old witch never sickened. The outlaws roamed in bands here and there, worrying the countryside like fleas, growing fractious and snapping like dogs. Some had killed, he knew that. Yet he was here, and his murderer was in the world beyond, and here he was safe.

Burnet stood up and stretched every limb, each in turn like a hawk, then went outside and walked about in the clearing. The rain had stopped and the air was brightening. Unfair, he thought for the millionth time, who wants me dead? Unfair. He swallowed and a lump in his throat went away. He did not know what he missed, though often he wept for it.

Bayardine was stacking wood peacefully, smiling as if remembering something. His dog nosed about at a distance.

I would like, thought Burnet, yawning, to be sitting down to eat from a loaded table. I would like to drink ale by the fire. I would like to go where I wish and live a life of ease.

He felt tightly coiled, like a snake. His muscles were hardening. His face, when he saw it in puddles, was stark and heavy. He wondered what day it was.

When the horn blew, he knew at once that something was wrong. It never came two days running. Bayardine listened, stiffening. Burnet, listening too with open mouth and distant eyes, felt a chill. They never listen, the fools never listen to me, he thought. I try to tell them but . . . he did not know why but knew that he must, and went up to Bayardine and gestured, raising his shoulders and hands.

Bayardine ignored him. 'My cloak's wet,' he said. 'Is the fire up?' He looked at the sky, then smiled. 'Ha,' he said, 'an outing.'

Burnet followed him into the hut and watched him blow up the fire and spread his cloak out to dry upon his bed. It began to steam, and a sharp, animal smell rose up from it.

'I am summoned,' said Bayardine gaily.

Burnet looked sullen. He grew sick of trying to express himself without a voice. The fools never stopped to look. He might as well be an island. More and more he wandered alone beyond the ramparts, hating and loving the great trees that gave him shelter. Sometimes he thought of dead Darby, who had loved solitude and paid a price for it. Sometimes he dreamed of the sea and woke tasting salt on his lips. He felt haunted. Sometimes he was dying for someone to touch him, anyone, and woke burning in the middle of the night. Bayardine slept peacefully. Nothing disturbed his dreams. Bayardine was probably mad. He had this woman he thought no-one had ever seen, around whom he'd erected a myth of romance. The joke was that everyone knew he was an old woman's toy, bought with baubles. Damned if I'd run to a call like that, Burnet thought. But

THE UNMAKING ❖ 115

why so soon, he saw her only yesterday? Damned if I'd go.

They do it in that house. The woman there looks out for them. Damned if I'd risk it. Suppose her husband—

Perhaps she's a widow.

Still, I wouldn't risk it, she must have kin.

The horn two days running is wrong. Is he mad? I wouldn't go. Yes, he is mad. We're all mad here. Still, he's survived this long, he cannot be such a fool. Look at the great thing, the great baby stuffing his bread in his mouth. What a birth, the fire! I would not be him.

Bayardine sat beside his steaming cloak, sucking his fingers.

Something is going to happen. I feel it, I feel it.

Burnet walked to Bayardine and gripped his arm and looked at him closely. Surprised, Bayardine looked down at his hand then up at his face, with eyes quite empty. The whorled skin had a polished look.

'What?' asked Bayardine. 'Get off me.'

God forgive me, Bayard, I am terrified and I do not know why.

'Get off me,' said Bayardine, scowling and shaking his arm. 'What are you ranting about? Why is all this wood damp? Here, you go that side and blow underneath and we might be able to get the thing going. My bones are cold. This'll be a stinking winter. You mind you wash your feet, Burnet. You stink the place out sometimes. Darby was just the same. My feet never smell.'

Burnet blew the fire up, then lay on his bed again and faced the wall. To hell with him. The dreams descended once more and he drifted in and out of them aimlessly for a while. She will come shining into my hut, smelling of spring, and she will throw out the darkness like old water, she will lie down on top of me—his eyes rolled beneath their flickering lids, his own hand caressed himself. We are walking into the woods. We throw ourselves down on the ground. Oh, she is—

Bayardine was shaking out his cloak. The smoke from the fire billowed and he laughed. Burnet sneezed and he laughed more.

Burnet rose up onto one elbow, bleary. Bayardine was combing his hair with a greasy silver comb.

'What do you think, Burnet?' he said, leaning forward, the livid burn shiny. 'Handsome, aren't I?' He stood up, pulling the cloak about him and flinging the hood over his head. 'Now—' He laughed. 'See the forest part before me!'

He stooped his head and went outside.

Burnet sat up too quickly and his vision clouded. By the time he stumbled out Bayardine had gone. Surely this was only fancy, but the knot of unease tightened in his belly. He had nothing to do. He ran back inside and got his coat and knife and set off, found himself dogging Bayardine and the hound through the quiet dripping forest. Now I'm as good a ghost as he is, Burnet thought. He's getting careless. Protected! Anyone could pick him off. Fate's nurtured him, can throw him away.

But an image came into his mind then of another figure still, dogging him as he dogged Bayardine, and he stopped for a moment and listened. There was nothing. He looked back once. The leaves were still. Continuing, the small fear that he had felt all day began to thicken and rise in him, slow and insistent, curling like smoke. It sharpened him. The sound of his own swallowing crackled in his ear.

Soon, he thought, I will have watched him come and go in safety, I'll beat him back home and be there on my bed as if I'd never moved, and he'll say perhaps, 'Look, Burnet, look what *I* have.'

The figure ahead moved steadily, without haste, the hound running on in front. They feared nothing. Oh, but I do, I do, Burnet thought, and at some point the journey became dream-like. He felt as if he were walking on the bed of the sea. The wood climbed. Bayardine vanished, but Burnet knew anyway where he was going. He did not want to reach the top of the climb. Stupid imaginings! But what if it were not? Why had he not brought help? Burnet, the one without a voice, Burnet who weeps sometimes. Who'd listen?

Self-pity overcame him. Silence was killing him. Sometimes he wondered what his voice had been like. Perhaps he sang. No music in the world was more wonderful than the human voice, he thought. Death came severally. His voice had died, but not he, yet the one who'd used the voice was undoubtedly dead. Each little death brought with it fear of a greater. Bayardine thinks he is immortal. That, thought Burnet, is a terrible sin!

He pushed on to the top and found a sheltered place on the lip of the wood, from where he could see Bayardine descending through a long bank of bracken. The beck formed a pool below and the house was round the next outcrop of rock, separated from them by a little field. The sky was very clear and there was birdsong.

What shall I do now? he thought. Why have I come? There he is in the open and I can do nothing. At the pool's edge, Bayardine paused for a moment and even put back his hood to look at himself in the still water. The man is mad, with so much cover all around. The hound sat scratching itself nearby. Man and dog showed as little concern as if they were at their own fire-side, and he realised at once that it was familiarity that bred Bayardine's recklessness. They had done this so many times. Of course, he thought, he was expecting the call, no doubt it had been spoken of. And he was relieved suddenly, believing himself to be wrong, and laughed without a sound.

There was a movement in the branches arching above his head and he looked up. A hawk had just alighted there. For a long moment he looked at the bird. Deeper still, the fear returned.

He heard a single cold whisper and looked down.

Bayardine was running backwards from the water, bending double, his hands at his middle. The hound skipped along with him as if it were a game. Bayardine sat down heavily like a baby unsteady on its feet.

Burnet knew the arrow was there before he saw it, sticking straight out from Bayardine's waist just above the silver buckle. Whoever had fired it must be here in these trees, below and to the right of him. His mouth dried up and his breath stopped.

Bayardine looked down at his fingers gripping the arrow, then up at the trees. He was grinning, and the hound licked the burned side of his face. A second whisper, a second arrow hit him in the chest, the impact flattening him. The hound ran around him, barking with excitement. Bayardine did not cry out, perhaps could not, but a terrible panic ensued. His head kept trying to rise and snapping back, his body arched, his legs pumped. His face, when it could be seen, was horribly distorted, mad with rage or fear or pain, and the hound kept leaping, dancing, poking its long nose into his face, running from head to feet and back again with little nervous yelps.

He did not make a good death. Not as good as my own, the thought came, but Burnet did not know where from. There was a sound in his ears, as if someone had run a hundred miles and was dying from it. It was himself, the breath rattling in his chest. He thought that he would faint, sat down and buried his face in his arms, stuffing his mouth full of his sleeve. Darkness closed in and fear raked him till he shook with sobs. It was not Bayardine he cried for but himself, dying, murdered, left alone with the blood running away into the leaf mould, bubbling in his nose and mouth, and the little purple flowers lying scattered by his hand. He was a child again, miserable, abandoned, crying, What have I done? Don't leave me alone to die! I meant no harm. Oh God, have mercy, mercy, I swear I meant no harm. Not death. Please, not death.

When he opened his eyes and raised his head, the leaves all around him were very clear. He stood up. His knees were weak. Below, Bayardine lay still, his head on one side and both knees bent outwards. His hands still clutched the arrow at his middle. Burnet felt sick. Bayardine, he thought. Everyone dies but not Bayardine—I am protected! Your feet stink, Burnet, take them out of my way! Can you talk, son? Know me, do you? What do they say about me where you come from? Bayardine. Demon.

Two horsemen came riding from the shelter of the trees into the open, horribly close. He saw their backs. A broad, heavy man with iron-grey hair rode a big bay horse. The other was the bowman. Dressed all in brown, he sat stiff-backed upon a powerful grey whose great flanks swayed as they descended the bank towards the pool.

Burnet knew this man at once and the sight of him turned his guts to water. There should be a hawk on the man's wrist. Why? Burnet's head ached. It was too much. He stuffed his fingers in his mouth. His face, he thought, if he turns, what will his face be? What is he? God, God, take this awful dream away. Let me go home. Me and Bayardine eating our supper. I know this man. Lord God, I do know him, and I hate him, I hate him.

My murderer.

Burnet wanted to run down the brown bracken bank, screaming, Why? Why? Why? What had I done?

The men reached level ground and dismounted, leaving their peaceful horses to graze above the pool while they stepped down to the place where Bayardine's body lay. They beat away the hound, which stood at a distance trembling cravenly. Burnet could see the shaking of its thin legs. 'God help me,' he tried to whisper. This dream was hellish. All of it had happened before, the stink of death, the grey horse champing the grass, the man turning his head to look at me, no mercy in those eyes.

What have you done, you silly lad?

Burnet saw the man's face. It looked peevish. Bayardine was

a fool. Who am I? Death's Angel. Death's very sweet and lovely Angel. Not you, Bayardine. Him. What is he? What *can* he be, killing me and now you? For what? Does he need a reason? Not if he's Death, pure and simple. Prove me wrong, Bayardine, please. Get up now and take him by the throat.

Bayardine lay still.

He's come back for me, thought Burnet, and turned and fled, startling the hawk, which shrieked and flew away. The terror of death pursued, beating the bushes for him, but he did not look back as he ran, fast as the undergrowth would allow, panic chafing his breast.

Did you hear that?'

'What?'

'A hawk,' said Hugh, thinking of Phoebe, 'sounded like a hawk.'

Harlock ignored this, letting his bag slip to the ground and bending with a vague air over the sprawled heap wearing his good cloak.

'Something startled it.' Hugh looked around. 'What could have startled it?'

'I heard nothing.' Harlock's voice was precise and measured.

It should have been easier, Hugh was thinking. After the first, it should be easier. But when he looked closely at Bayardine's parti-coloured face, with one eye staring straight at heaven as if horrors were there and the other skenning outwards towards the meaty flap of skin that hung over it, he knew that it was not. 'He is dead?' he asked. 'He is really dead?'

'Of course he is.' Harlock, his face composed, then kicked Bayardine so hard in the side that the whole body jumped. Hugh started back a little, and a cold bead of sweat rolled down at the corner of his eye. He was still elated from the kill but knew obscurely that Harlock's ferocity was inapt.

Both stared fascinated at the big burned face that registered no outrage at such insult.

'Fine cloak,' said Hugh.

Harlock laughed and kicked again, so hard this time that the neck snapped back and a great exhalation left the body. Hugh blinked.

Harlock looked up and smiled at him. 'Better this way,' he said softly. 'No barbarism. Do you know what the law would have done with him?'

Hugh nodded.

'He fared better than the rest of his kin.'

But Hugh was thinking of how he'd raised John Heron and set his back against a tree, how the boy's eyes had slithered upwards, white like the flesh of a fish, how sweet and childlike his throat was before the blade bit, and he remembered the sounds the blood made. These things came so willingly to his mind.

Harlock stooped and removed Bayardine's fingers gently, one by one, from their grip upon the arrow, then pulled it out. It did not come easily.

'See,' he said, holding it aloft for calm inspection, 'the blood is thicker here.'

The broad tip of the arrow dripped. Hugh's gullet rose. Shame, he thought. What? Sickened at a little blood?

The second arrow, from the heart region, came easier. 'And here it is thinner,' said Harlock.

Hugh raised his eyes to Harlock's face and stared. The man's eyes were small and grey and absolutely empty. Hugh found himself afraid, creepingly, there in the full light of day. Harlock saw his fear and smiled again.

'Trembling?' he said. 'Why? Do you know what you have done? You have killed Bayardine. Think of that. Everyone wants to kill Bayardine. Bayardine is a thief and a murderer and a fornicator. You have fulfilled the law, that is all.'

'*We* have fulfilled the law,' said Hugh very stiffly. 'Yours was the intelligence, mine merely the execution.' We are both sober, he thought. That's what is wrong. We cannot be at ease together. The man is not mad, he's just sober.

'Your knife,' Harlock said briskly.

'My knife,' Hugh repeated blankly.

'Your knife, your knife.' An edge of irritation crept into Harlock's sober voice. 'Mine is not so keen. The outlaw's knife.'

Hugh did not immediately reply.

'The knife you gave me?' he said then, hearing how stupid his voice sounded. He'd lost his grip on the situation.

Harlock scowled and his heavy face flushed. 'Oh, come on, man,' he said, 'I want to borrow your knife.'

'Why?' asked Hugh. Execution was one thing, butchery another.

Harlock looked up at him and said nothing for some time. 'Why?'

'I want his head,' said Harlock with faint incredulity.

It was cold. Oh, Lord God, Lord God, thought Hugh, I wish I were home. At Caddenhope, by the fire, in the old days. 'Use your sword!' he said sharply, and he had never spoken so to Harlock before.

'No!' Harlock was grim and urgent. 'Your knife! I want it. It fits. An outlaw's knife for an outlaw's head.' He laughed. 'I want his head. A trophy, you see. What an ugly great head he has! Look the other way if you're squeamish.'

'Oh, man,' said Hugh softly, 'this is foul.'

But he drew the outlaw's knife from its beautiful sheath and handed it anyway to Harlock, who dropped to one knee at once and seized the long yellow locks. Hugh turned away. He could watch the decapitation of any beast but not this. There was no sound till the hacking of bone, and Harlock grunting with exertion, then a crack and the sound of heavy tearing. A ragged mess, Hugh thought. He would have unmade a deer with more care. What is this? I never exulted so over John Heron.

The afternoon was drawing in and the sky had begun to fade a little. Cloud shadow moved across the bracken. Bayardine's dog slunk quaking on the edge of the forest, its thin worm of a tail pressed tight between its legs. A few birds were coming in to roost. Harlock breathed hard.

'I have it,' he said, standing with a grunt. 'Here.'

Hugh turned. Harlock had wiped the knife and now held it out, the blade in his bloody gloved hand. From the other hung the good thick hessian bag, heavily weighted. There were dark stains on his sleeve and the front of his cloak. Hugh took the knife and sheathed it quickly, his mouth prim.

'Let us go, for the love of God,' he said, and his eyes could not but fall upon the body, which was no more than just a man without a head, preposterous and ridiculous with its clumsy knees and foolish hands. A silent crimson stream spilled out of the neck and spread through the slick grass, shining brightly before the rich earth soaked it up.

Hugh walked quickly to his horse, mounted and waited, biting the skin inside his mouth and clenching his thighs so that the mare trod restlessly. Harlock followed and hung the bag from his saddle, mounted and set off without a word. It hung down by his leg as they rode, rolling against his knee from time to time, but he seemed not to care.

Well, I have a fairish new piece of land now, thought Hugh. Two men now, two fornicators. Or so he tells me. It went dark quickly these nights, the days seeming weak. 'Well, a man is but an animal,' he whispered to Serafina, her patient grey head nodding on before him in the growing gloom. But when they reached Ellwin and met in the hallway the lingering aroma of meat stewed in verjuice, a sickness exploded in his chest and his forehead sweated.

This is more than it seems, he thought. All this is more than it seems.

Sim stood uneasily, waiting for instruction. Harlock sat on the edge of the bed holding between his legs a bag that smelt of blood and was darkening at the base. He'd brought meat into the room. What is strange? thought Sim. Out hunting with Rennock all afternoon, missing supper, calling for water from behind the curtains of his bed, washing, changing his clothes at this hour of the day. I blew the horn. What of it? Why does he tell me nothing?

Has he killed? Some old wife? Because of me. No, not him.

'Where is your mistress?'

Now. *Now* he would beat her.

'Sewing in her room.'

'What? Still?'

'She asked for a light,' said Sim. 'She said she particularly wanted to finish something.'

Harlock nodded, looking down sideways to the floor. Sim knew now what was strange. Harlock looked thoughtful. 'Sim,' he said.

'Sir?'

Harlock was silent for several minutes. Then he said, 'Nothing. You may go.'

Sim bowed and withdrew.

'Yes,' said Harlock to himself quietly, nodding. 'Yes. Yes.' His fingers played restlessly with the neck of the bag. For a moment he looked down at it blankly, then lifted it onto his knees, lightly fingering the outside of it before standing and placing it over one shoulder so that it hung heavily against his back as he left the room and walked down steps and along a flagged passage that led to his wife's chamber.

The room smelt pleasantly of new rushes and blazed with candles, by whose light she stitched swiftly and diligently at the pure white silk, elevated a little in her thronely chair.

'This is wasteful,' he said, indicating the candles.

She looked up briefly then down again. 'Where were you at supper?' she asked.

Harlock marvelled that she did not see the change in him. He felt his power rising like a sun while hers diminished, and was irresistably drawn to the game. And what a game it would be, and how he would shudder at the horror of it even as he played.

'Did you not know?' he said. 'I've been hunting with Rennock.'

The bag touched the back of his knees and he wanted to giggle.

'Well,' she said, 'you have been keeping very much alone.' She sighed and turned her work over. 'Does the tooth still hurt?'

He damned her for reminding him of the pain in his head, which had grown constant in his life, like days of rain.

'Aren't you going to ask me about the quarry?' he said too loudly and she looked up again, irritated and a little surprised at his tone, wondering what he was angry about now.

'What is the matter with you?' she asked sharply.

He'd wanted to say something fine about how tender was the quarry, something for her to think about afterwards when she had begged him for her life and he had spared it, but instead he stepped further into the room with a smile he felt was ghastly. 'I've brought you a gift,' he said.

She frowned. It was so unlikely an occurrence that it raised more fear than expectation. She saw touches of blood on his hose.

'The *present,* madam,' he said grandly, and started to laugh. The laugh disturbed her for it was not his own but something altogether higher and more foolish, and a little finger of ice touched the nape of her neck and made her glad of all the candles.

'A ball,' he said, 'for you to play with.'

'A ball?'

'Look what you have made me do!'

He brought the bag from behind his back and let its heavy

burden, shaggy and yellow and red, fall from its open neck and roll swiftly to the foot of her chair, where it harboured for a moment in her trailing skirts before rebounding a little. She gave an ugly, ragged cry, jumping up and jarring the chair, kicking out with her feet uselessly, then scuttled back against the wall and jammed herself into the corner with both hands pushing hard at her gaping mouth. Above them, her eyes were stricken. She drew in a long, painful breath, like someone recovering from drowning.

The lips of the head were drawn back and its brown side teeth showed. There was nothing in the eyes, nothing at all, and the colour had drained from the unburned flesh. Harlock felt a horrible urge to go and jump on this object, so empty and so full, a rotten fruit that would explode on impact.

She stared. His lovely hair, she thought. What have they done to his lovely hair? Browning yellow at the roots, it bushed out dryly where the blood had not soaked. The rest was dark red spirals that had painted a mess across the new rushes and on the creamy hem of her gown. Some trailing ends stuck fast across his face, and one had lodged along the rim of his good eye, bloodying the egg-like ball.

May came forward slowly and kneeled, horribly fascinated. Her hand went out and gently touched the hair that was dry, and her eyes became compassionate. The strand of hair, a thin red elver, moved from the eye.

She jumped up again, shuddering all over and batting at her skirts with both hands as if worms were invading her from the floor below, ran up and down before the window with tiny steps and gave small crying gasps, as if merely very exasperated. Harlock watched her intently.

Then she stood still, putting her hands to either side of her head and swaying, her lips drawing back in dreadful similarity to those of the head, looking at him. For a moment he was touched by a greater horror than any he had so far experienced, for her eyes were naked and begging, just as he had intended; she had never turned such a look on him before, and he wished desperately that nothing had ever changed. He did not know what to do with this look.

'No,' she said, her voice deep. 'No, no, no, no, please, please, please . . .'

Her eyes wandered round the room, everywhere but to the head, coming back to Harlock in the end.

'What?' he said.

'I didn't speak,' she said.

He laughed.

She screamed once, piercingly, cutting off the sound as if with a scythe.

Harlock heard footsteps in the passage and ran to the door. 'It's nothing!' he said peremptorily to the anxious faces of servants approaching. 'She fell asleep over her seam and had a bad dream, you are not needed.'

The faces hovered, white, idiotic. Sim was with them. His mouth hung open and he looked as if he'd just woken up, ruffled, weak about the eyes. No-one moved. Harlock resisted an urge to roar at them. 'Away with you!' he said, trying to make his voice avuncular but hearing how he sounded like a drunken man rebuffing an offer of help. And I am sober, he thought, sober as milk, and laughed aloud. All the little faces looked afraid, none more so than Sim. One by one they went out in the darkness, like stars.

Harlock went back inside and slammed the door. She was standing with her arms down by her sides, her face empty as if she'd just been slapped. That awful bloody thing lay there in her safe room drawing all the candlelight, bright as a mask.

'You are old,' he said baldly, loud, to be sure that she heard. 'What was it? His youth? Is that it? Slobbering over that?'

She did not move.

'It can't have been his beauty! Don't you see how ridiculous you were? Are you mad?' His voice grew stronger, more sure. 'You have shamed yourself intolerably. Do you understand? Might as well have gone as a whore to the whole scabby lot of them. Do you see? *Do you see?*'

She showed no sign of having heard and he laughed, a clipped, barking sound. 'I have saved you,' he said. 'Do you see that? I have actually saved you. You would have gone on and on and . . .'

'What have you done?' she whispered. 'How did you know?'

'What does it matter?' he cried, 'Sim told me,' becoming mad because he did not know what to do now that everything he'd planned had happened just so, and the thing was growing fouler and fouler and the pain of his tooth was rising like a thread of flame.

'Sim?' she echoed faintly.

'Sim! Sim!' he rapped, as if she were stupid. 'Oh, believe me, he had no idea who it was you met there. Thank God! Your shame is still hidden. Rennock killed him, but doesn't know why.' He laughed again.

'Rennock?' she whispered.

'Rennock. His was the honour,' he said grandly, and a short laugh stuck in his throat. 'The rest of him's draining into Ellwin Beck.'

May looked full at him, like a sleepwalker, then down at last, and her eyes sharpened with a grief she made no attempt to hide. Then tears came. Harlock watched in disbelief, horrified, as she slowly stooped and slowly took the ugly face between her hands.

'There, my sweet,' she said softly, and lifting the sodden head as if it were a rare treasure, let it nestle on one arm at her breast, one matronly hand patting it to rest. The filthy locks hung long and tangled. 'There,' she said, and kissed the lousy parting of its hair. A torrent followed, the more horrible because it was silent as it shook her, as if some dreadful killing ague had descended in the space of a second, making her ancient and unrecognisable.

His scalp crawled. He fought an urge to run from the room. Blood dripped down the cream of her gown and he wanted to wipe away the sight of her. He walked about the room taking control, restoring order with the staunchness of his voice: 'Waste, waste, all waste,' he said, and blew out the candles one by one till only two remained, flickering feverishly.

The thing was only a ball now.

He stood near the door. There was no sound. There never would be again. The calm was sudden, unnatural, and that chilled him too. His wife was mad and the world had changed forever. She moved to her chair, lifting the white silk shirt and tucking it about her ghastly armful, then sat down with it, rocking slightly. She seemed to him lost in an immense bovine stupidity of grief.

Fury saved him. 'Are you mad?' he thundered, pacing about with his hand on the hilt of his sword. 'May! This is horrible, horrible, woman! Fawning on it! On filth! You are disgusting, vile—you *are* mad!—With him? With that! Oh, *Christ,* it's monstrous!—Tell me—tell me—tell me, woman, why I should not kill you? Now! Tell me!'

She laughed softly.

'Tell me!'

She lifted her face and he drew back. 'Bayardine is my son,' she said.

'I will kill you.' He spoke so quietly that she could not hear.

'He is my son,' she repeated.

'It would be kinder to kill you,' he said very gently. Her face was a lapse of memory. 'Leave here, now, tonight, go anywhere, this is worse than blasphemy. You were possessed.'

'Listen!'

'He has turned your brain. Oh yes! And indeed he was young enough to be your son, but—'

'Listen!'

Harlock gaped at her.

'I was a girl. Later, I married you. Only the blood counts, that's what you say. The blood. It was noble.' Two thin tears rolled down her wide, pale cheeks, but her features were still and her voice firm.

'You are deluded,' he said, taking one step forward. 'His mother was the witch. You were virgin when we married, or I would have—'

'Killed me?' she supplied blankly.

'No, no!'

'Do. Will you now? Do you think it matters? Do you know what a fool you are, my lord?' Her eyes were quite steady though they overflowed from time to time. She settled Bayardine more firmly in the crook of her arm.

'It was the third son of a baron,' she said, 'from Scotland. Noble, you see.'

Harlock scowled.

'From Scotland,' she repeated. 'He was travelling with his brother from France to his home, and we gave them lodging for a time. So.'

'Lying.'

'My mother knew of it.'

'You are lying.'

'I was always big. It wasn't so hard to hide the signs.'

Harlock cried out and turned around as if to leave but turned again and stared in fascination at her hand gently stroking the head.

'Ellen Fuller read palms. My mother took me there—' A flicker passed across her face. 'What have you done to her?' she cried.

'Who?' he whispered.

'What have you done to her?'

'Who?' he shouted. 'The hag by the beck? Nothing yet.'

'She is under my protection!' she said, her voice gave out and she bowed her head over and cried into Bayardine's hair.

Harlock could not stand it. 'No!' he said. 'You are telling tales! What are you telling me?'

'Truth!' she gasped, raising her face. 'You will listen! If any were killed it should be me! *I* gave him life, *I* gave him away, *I* put the fear of discovery on the woman and all her household. Is this not blood enough for you?'

Harlock raised his arm but did not approach her. He had no words.

'He was born there,' she said. 'In that house. I had him an hour and they took him. She said she'd found a good foster mother in Herndale, a woman whose husband had died and her baby was born dead. She had four others, but she loved him the best. Oh, she was good to him! We made sure of that.'

'Are you telling me—'

'Bayard, I called him. I was very young. I thought it was a pretty name.'

'—that you have never—'

'Not a peasant's name at all.'

'—that you have never played the whore—'

'Two years and I did not see him. It never happened, my mother said.'

'I am speaking!'

She frowned. It was just the look she had when he spoke too quietly for her to hear, and he wanted to laugh and say, 'Well, May, what was all that about?' and she would stand up, smiling and putting her work away, and there would be truce.

'Are you telling me,' he said in measured tones, 'that you have never played the whore since we were wed?'

'That is what I am telling you,' she said, the same, 'if you will listen.'

Harlock walked to the bed and sat down. Yesterday morning, the world was sane. His lips were dry. A drink, he thought, before I die, a drink.

'Two years,' she said. 'And then one day I saw him. She was a brisk, busky little woman going down the road with a basket and a gaggle of dark-haired children. And a great fair baby. Mine.'

She looked into Bayardine's face. 'Mine. He was bonny then,' she said wonderingly, 'such a beautiful manchild. Oh yes, mine! I was married to you. I had not conceived.' Then she was silent for so long that Harlock thought it was over.

He looked about. Now, he thought, I can put all this to rights. For what he became I cannot be blamed. I will forgive. I will make her see that I have done no wrong. Why, she was only a girl. Girls are foolish.

But she looked at him again with her pale, weak eyes, the rims red. 'Wasn't she a fool though?' she said.

'Who?' he asked, his voice a croak.

'His mother. Two mothers, we used to tell him. Aren't you a lucky boy? She was well paid, you see. She had no need to sell her gifts. But she could see, you know. That much I'm sure was true. She could hold your hands and tell you why your head ached so. She did not like me. Well, I did not blame her for that. See me appearing laden with gifts! At Ellen's house, we always met there. But she never said a word. How could she? Years.' She laughed. 'Don't you remember? What! Going to see your mother again? Oh, but I am sick for Herndale, the loveliest spot! Oh yes! And he grew as high as my shoulder.'

She looked at Harlock.

'You did not know him. He changed. After the fire.'

'The fire,' said Harlock, and swallowed. 'It was not my

fault. I could not stop it. You cannot blame me for that.'

'No,' she said, 'not you. Me. My doing. Mine entirely.' Her eyes closed and her throat worked.

'Not me, not you,' he said, jumping up and standing at a loss. 'Have sense! We none of us command the weather!'

'Oh no,' she said softly. 'None of us do. Do you remember? Snow at Whitsun. And the rain, on and on and on and everything rotting, everything rotting, winter, everyone starving, the poor grey creatures! Not she though! Not she and her children, not she and that big golden lad with the roses in his cheeks! Why, what else could have kept them so well if it wasn't witchcraft? I did! I did!' A fit of tears thickened her voice and drowned her eyes. 'They wanted for nothing! She was very well paid! Well paid! The fool! She should have been careful! All that I gave, all I sent, all I—didn't she know her own neighbours? What was I? How could I know? They were not my people! And you—you—you said—if these people will meddle with fire, well, they will be burned. All of them! And he was gone!' She sobbed. 'I thought he was dead.'

Harlock stood still, his mouth open. He remembered. Her mother had died soon after. A week in bed she'd spent grieving for the old woman, so he'd thought, ruining the fine sheets.

'And then some time—oh, I don't know, many months,' said May in wonder, 'sewing on the terrace, I heard a horn blowing very softly from the edge of the forest, I remember, and I woke up and lifted my head to listen . . .

'I could hear well then,' she said.

There was a long silence.

Harlock licked his lips audibly. She had closed Bayardine's eyes and he looked peaceful now, as if merely asleep and quite unaware of his lack of a body. Harlock felt an urge to laugh. His voice, when it came, was hoarse and belligerent, though he had intended to speak gently.

'You should have told me. I would not have killed your son. If I had known—how could I know if you did not tell me?—what was I to think, seeing you and—what would any man think?' He felt that he was babbling.

She laughed. 'Tell you?' she said. 'That I had a bastard? An *outlaw* bastard? Those *vermin*.' She laughed again. Then she said, 'Whatever he did or became, I am completely to blame,' and dropped her head and started to sing in a cracked, hoarse voice, some old baloo balilly.

Harlock threw open the door and fled in terror. There was madness in her now. Near his own door, hot and sick, he stood shuddering, clawing bleakly at his eyes. I have killed an outlaw, nothing more. No, not I, Rennock! It is no crime to kill an outlaw. The judge and all would say so. No crime, no crime. 'No crime,' he said aloud.

William appeared at the head of the stairs, a spaniel pup under one arm. 'Father?' he said uncertainly. 'Are you all right?'

Harlock stared at him, amazed. Here was his silly son, here his door, here about him the house in which he'd been born. All changed. He spat to one side. He'd never liked William. Never liked him. Thought it was her weak blood. Jesus, the Scot must have been a big brute.

'Father?' came William's voice, concerned.

Harlock laughed. This long and dreadful day was not yet over. He needed to drink the good claret, then he would see clearly again.

Sim ran through the house, afraid that the monstrous head would appear and snap at him from the shadows. A head had haunted his childhood, that of his own father, cut off for treason. Another would join it. Together they'd pursue him to the end. He jarred his elbow on the wall and cried out as if the thing had

touched him. He had heard, he had seen through the crack in
the door. Sim knew all that the great folk did. He'd seen the filth
on their fine holland sheets.

Reaching his bed he lay curled defensively, getting his breath
and closing his eyes, seeing on the darkness a long smear of
blood on the rushes. He felt sick, as if blood was running down
his very soul. What would she do? She would come, bringing
the thing and holding it up so that it could look at him, and say,
'Sim, you have told tales.'

He sat alert with a cry as if a knife had poked him. What have
I done? he thought. I only meant her to get a beating. That
would have done. I would have been happy with just one
glimpse. Not this. Not this. His heart hammered. In the midst
of fear there was glee. I have changed the lives of great folk, he
thought. It's not my fault. I'm only a servant, everyone knows
a servant can have no bearing on anything. All I did was tell the
truth. Is there any blame in that?

This was a foul, cruel world. Servants died, swatted like flies,
when the affairs of great folk foundered. Sim smiled grimly. He
had caused the son of his mistress to die and she knew it.

He got up and went to the window and saw how the full
moon's light had given everything a silver hue. He could not
imagine the morning that would follow this night. Why, he
thought with some surprise, Bayardine was William's brother.

Belle, dear,' said a voice in the passage outside her door.

She'd been watching the full moon from the window and thought at first that the voice was in her mind. Soon she would go to bed and lie awake for an hour or two as she always did, watching the candle burn low.

'Belle, dear,' it said again, the same patient tone, and she turned her head, blinking sleepily, a little annoyed at the disturbance. They intruded enough upon her.

'Come in,' she called impatiently to her mother-in-law, wondering why she did not knock or walk in.

After a pause, May said: 'You come to the door.'

Belle frowned. She went to the door and opened it and saw May standing far back in the shadows, a lantern in one hand, the other bundled up under a heavy mantle that she held close about her as if she were going out.

'I am sorry,' May said. 'I need your help.' The stiffness in her voice was unnatural.

'Why, what's the matter?' Belle reached out and took her by the arm, trying to draw her into the room, but she was immovable.

'Will you come with me?' May asked in the same stiff tone, 'Will you? An hour or two, Belle, that is all. Your company, please, Belle, your company just for a little, please.'

Belle stepped back, disturbed. May was an amiable, light woman and this was not her. This was so different, though the face was the same, that the thought of possession came into her mind and made her afraid.

'Come forward!' she said peremptorily, amazed at her own boldness. 'Let me see you.'

May took a step or two. Her eyes were red and miserable. Belle touched her again, fear changing to pity. 'What's happened?' she said. May shook her head.

'Tell me!'

She went on shaking her head, opening and closing her eyes and mewing faintly through closed lips, and Belle was torn. Go away, she wanted to shout, leave me in peace, I am going to bed. There's enough grief in the world without this. Go away and I'll believe I never saw you. I am dreaming. Poor Mother! Whatever it is, I'll help you, but there's nothing I can do, I'm too weak, something terrible has happened and I don't know what it is and none of it is my affair anyway.

'Enough!' she said, afraid. 'If you want help, you must come in and sit down and tell me everything or I can do nothing. Please!' She spoke more gently. 'You are frightening me. Please, come in and tell me. It will not seem so terrible—'

But May moved back into the shadows. 'How can I?' she whispered angrily. 'You wouldn't believe me. You'd tell me I was mad. How can I? If you knew—' She stopped to catch her breath. Then she laughed, and the change in her again was so great that Belle shrank back. 'Believe the impossible,' May said. 'Can you? No! I cannot believe it myself, and I am wholly to blame.'

'What do you want?' asked Belle faintly.

May laughed.

'What do you want?' she asked more loudly, becoming irritated.

'Belle,' said May, 'I have something very strange to tell you.'

'Jesus, it is cold out here,' said Belle, shivering. 'Why don't you come in?'

'Well now, if I came in . . .' said May, looking aside and

smiling. 'No! Listen. I'll tell you.' She thought awhile, then said, 'William was not my only living child.'

There was a silence.

'Yes,' said Belle.

'Are you surprised?'

Belle did not speak.

'I had a son,' said May, 'before I was wed. He was fostered on a peasant woman.'

Belle heard sounds in the house, the distant closing of a door, a faint burst of man's laughter. May's eyes were on her face. What am I to say? she thought. It could easily have happened to me. What shall I say? Mother, I understand, I'm a sinner too.

'I have seen him grow up not far from here,' said May.

Her! thought Belle. I never would have thought it of her. I wonder what she was like? Was it like the barn, me with John? Oh, John Heron, I do wish he'd go away.

Incubus.

'He's dead!' said May. Her mouth opened wide.

Now we come to it.

'He's dead!'

'When?' she asked, awkward.

'Murdered! Now!' May looked as if she should be screaming and crying but no sound emerged.

Sweet Christ, what does she want from me? 'Oh, Mother,' she said, 'come in here, please come in here, lie down on my bed, please. You can rest, and I will—'

'No! I have to go out, I have to—'

'At this hour?'

'I cannot go alone,' she said petulantly, 'I am afraid, Belle, I am afraid. I am afraid of the—'

Belle turned away. Some death watch in a peasant's hut was demanded, it seemed. How could she refuse? And a part of her stirred, for it was a long time since she had ventured out in the night, a long time since she had peered into a peasant's hut.

'Does he know?' she asked. 'Your husband?'

May stared at her for a long time. The skin beneath her eyes was grey.

'It does not matter,' Belle said, turning into her room and gazing about in a vague manner as if she had just woken up. Well, she thought, I would not have slept anyway.

'My husband killed him,' said May.

Belle froze. Ah.

'No, not him. Your brother.'

Belle swung round. She is mad.

'I have cursed them!' said May. 'I have cursed them, Belle, to Hell. I have cursed, I have, I have cursed, I have cursed them!'

Belle stared at the weak, desperate eyes. Mad or drunk. Perhaps, after all, she and Harlock were suited to each other. This was a terrible family she'd fallen into! 'My brother?' she said. 'My brother has done nothing!'

'I dare not go alone at so late an hour. We must go very quietly, we must not take horses, no-one else must know of this. Listen, Belle, your brother and my husband have killed him and they have left him lying by Ellwin Beck all alone, and I cannot have him there so uncared for. I am not mad. All this is true.' The look in her eyes never changed, but she spoke with authority, as if she were giving orders for the running of the household.

'My brother has done nothing,' Belle repeated, wanting to cry and stamp her foot. People had no right to go mad so suddenly.

'An hour or two.' May came close to her and spoke deliberately up into her face with steady eyes and hard, pale lips. A faint, sweet, sickly smell came into Belle's nostrils. 'I have shown you kindness since you came into my house. I have pitied your homesickness. Now. The servants are all instructed to drink my husband's health. My maids are afraid. None must know of this anyway, least of all William. I have trusted you. Who else is there but you?'

Belle drew back. He has done nothing, Hugh has done nothing. If he did, there must have been a reason. Harlock made him do it!

'What can we do alone?' she asked hopelessly.

'There is a house near the beck,' said May. 'I know the people. They will help us bring him in. Understand, if he were yours—' Her brow crinkled. 'Would you leave him alone for the bloody wolves to—' She drew her breath in sharply and her mouth clamped shut.

Wolves. What are we to do? 'It is late,' Belle said weakly.

'Yes, it is late,' said May.

Belle turned back into her room and stood irresolute, looking about. Fear began to tap against her breast. This is how it was, she thought, getting up in the night, creeping down the stairs, out under the stars and across the yard. Once more. Just so, the parrot winking peacefully on the perch, the bed sleek and inviting. What else can I do?

In the passage May stood like a rock. She would never move again from the door. Belle put on her cloak and threw the hood over her head and went to stand beside her. May nodded. 'Good,' she said. Then they went down through the chilly stone maze of the house, out into the crisp November night.

May gave Belle the lantern to carry, though its light was eclipsed by the great round of the moon, glowing with an engorged fulness high above the forest. Then she bundled both her arms together under the heavy mantle, shivering against the cold, and for a long time they walked in silence, side by side. Belle was dazed. I am walking with a mad woman to find a dead man and bring him in. She almost laughed, or sang, or skipped a measure in order to break the spell. The moon looked dangerous, as if it might fall or burst and kill them with its cold fire. Killing? she thought. Hugh was not at supper. I should have gone to him at once and got the truth of this. But still, the night was beautiful! Walking to meet John Heron, an age ago. When I was young.

They walked for so long that she wondered if she'd slept and woke and slept again, and if she were sleeping now. The moon showed all the little blades of grass that passed beneath their pacing feet, treading away the land with entrancing steadiness. Somewhere a little stream gurgled. May shifted something under her mantle.

'What are you carrying?' Belle asked. Her voice was shockingly clear, a sound from the real world breaking into a dream.

May did not answer. 'I am very sorry for this, Belle,' she said after a while. 'I am very, very sorry for this. It was good of you to come.'

The land became rough and they did not speak again till they reached a high place from where they could see Ellwin Beck glittering in the moonlight, the forest black behind.

'Down there,' said May. 'Draining into Ellwin Beck.' The fear in her voice made Belle shiver. She looked at her mother-in-law and swallowed.

'What now?' she said too loudly. 'Surely we've walked more than an hour already. We should have ridden.' She did not mean to sound so heartless. If there's truth in any of it, she thought, it's true that she's in grief, and tears rose suddenly in her own eyes.

May said nothing. Her eyes had sharpened with a kind of excitement and she started off down the incline boldly. Belle followed. She looked in vain for signs of the house that May had mentioned, but there was nothing at all in the night but black outcrops of rock, the curtains of the forest drawn tight, and all around like ghostly voices, the whispering of a hundred tiny streams flowing down into the beck. Here and there a trickle showed silver.

At last they stood on the bright hushing bank of the beck and a fruitless search began. Belle lost all sense of time. She forgot the cold and the purpose of the search, up and down, up and down, but merely followed, delighting perversely in the humped bodies of boulders, the whisper of their skirts in the grass, and the night scents of herbage crushed beneath their feet. The cold walls of Ellwin were dead. I shall give her the slip, she thought dreamily, never go back, find some enchantment and grow wings and a snout and fly above the forest. And she stood yawning, looking up at the moon and wanting to howl at it.

'He isn't here!' May stopped short.

Belle awoke. 'No,' she said vaguely, 'no-one is here,' and went to stand by May, whose face crumpled.

'He isn't here!' May clapped one hand to her mouth, looking round in despair. The other hand stayed under her mantle.

'What are you carrying?' Belle asked. Wide awake now, more than she'd ever been, the cold returned and made her teeth chatter.

'My son, Belle.' May began to sob, turning this way and that and babbling. 'No demon, my son. Dreadful things they say of him. Where is he? All alone somewhere and the damned crows at him! Oh, Bayard! Poor little Bayard!'

'Bayard?' Belle tried to take her arm. 'Bayard?'

May looked at her and laughed. 'Bayardine,' she said. 'My son.'

She truly is mad, Belle thought. I must take her home.

'Bayardine,' said May, laughing again. 'Your face, Belle! Don't stare so! Have you been listening to stories, Belle? Bayardine, your brother-in-law.'

She turned into the moonlight and Belle saw that something dark had smeared on her face.

'What are those marks?' she asked.

But May ran from her, higher up the beck to where it pooled, and stood there looking this way and that, stepping here, there, mumbling with aggravation. Belle followed.

'But there is nothing—' she began.

May cried out and ran a little forward, falling to one knee and putting out a hand to pat the earth. 'Here,' she whispered.

'What?' said Belle, afraid.

'Here,' said May in some agitation. 'Look.'

Belle came and knelt and saw that the grass was flattened and smeared over a large area.

'There's blood in the grass,' said May.

'What are we to do? I don't like it! Why are we here? Why did you call on me? What good can I do?' Belle jumped up and stepped back. Her heart hammered. She looked about. Night was like a watching face all around her. 'You said there was a house,' she said accusingly. 'Didn't you? Where is it? What can we do alone? If he was here, he's gone.'

'Where *is* he?' There was more anger in May than Belle had ever seen. 'This must not happen!' She scolded the ground. 'I will not have this!'

Belle shook her, horrified. 'You are going mad,' she said. 'Stop this now. Stop it. We must go to this house and rest. Where is it? Then we must—'

'You will do as you please,' said May bluntly as she gathered her skirts. 'I am going to find my son if I have to level this forest. You have a cold heart. Go, I will do without you.' She walked away. She had no fear.

Belle followed. 'Please,' she said desperately, 'wait, let us at least think what is the best thing to do. Have some understanding, you summon me so sudden with this talk of death and sons and my brother killing, and you bring me out here and I—'

'You think I'm mad,' said May. 'I am not. They have not taken him to the house. They would not dare. They've taken him into the forest. We will not find that place, we will not, we must storm it. Give me your hand.'

Dazed, Belle obeyed. The moonlight was strong and her eyes had grown so accustomed to the night that she felt she saw as clearly as she ever had. May's hand, the right, was filthy as a peasant's, the nails encrusted with some dark matter. 'What is this?' Belle asked.

May looked down at it and smiled.

'Sh,' she said, 'we must listen!'

Belle saw dark splashes on the pale hem of the gown that showed beneath May's mantle.

'Why, what have you been doing?' she asked. 'What is all that?'

May looked away. 'Blood, Belle dear,' she said, then opened her mouth very wide and hollooed like a man in the thick of the hunt. In that quiet place the sound was as horrible as it was laughable. She did it again.

Belle tore away her hand and tensed to run. 'What are you doing?' she hissed. 'You will get us killed!'

May stopped and turned to look at her as if she were a simpleton. 'We must announce ourselves,' she said. 'How else are we to find him?' She would have shouted again but Belle gripped her arm. 'The blood,' she said urgently, 'where did it come from? Are you hurt?'

'Hurt?' May said. 'Not me. Bayard.'

Belle turned cold.

May summoned her close and turned back a fold of her gown, and Belle saw a man's head, and the world was a terrible place where anything might happen. The shock took her breath. She suddenly noticed the sound of the beck, a good, clean sound, clear and forthright. This was the real Bayardine, this raging red hurt upon a pale face, these shiny blue lips. She imagined kissing the lips. John Heron came into her mind. She was starved.

I understand nothing, she thought.

'Do you see?' said May. 'What would you do? It is vile to

deprive a man of his head so that he can never be at peace! Vile!
It is the most brutish form of torture! I will have none of it for
him!'

I am looking at a man's head, Belle thought. So it is. He
nestled in something that shone softly like a ghostly halo, white
silk, almost blue. The night was something sticky, trapping her
like a fly in honey. She was still afraid but there was far more
now—yes, she thought with some surprise, I am enjoying this,
and the horror of it tightened her sinews, and an awful pain shot
through her heart. 'Oh, poor man,' she said, 'poor man,' and
began to cry.

May stared at her for a moment with open-mouthed surprise,
then she too cried.

A sound from the edge of the forest disturbed them and they
started and moved together.

'What was it? What was it?' May whispered. 'It was not clear.'

'Sh!' Belle strained her ears. 'Like a—' she began, but it came
again, unmistakably a low moan. 'Wolves?' she whispered.

'What?'

'Sh!'

'Something is moving,' said May.

'Christ,' said Belle, 'Christ.'

Something long and low padded away from the dark mass of
the trees.

'Tray!' May ran a few steps forward. 'Come, Tray! Darling
Tray!'

A large brindled hound came cringing towards her, dropping
to its belly and wriggling over the grass like a snake. Its head was
on one side, the long mouth gaping cravenly. Close by, it rolled
onto its back and pawed the air with graceful pointed feet, and
a thin, sad sound came from its snout.

'Good dog! Good dog, Tray! Poor Tray!'

The hound stood, neck stretched low, tail pressed into

the curve of its trembling back legs. His nose twitched.

'He smells blood,' said Belle.

He danced back suddenly as if they'd threatened, then turned and bolted towards the line of trees. May picked up her skirts and ran clumsily after him through the dim, tussocky grass. 'Tray!' she called.

'Oh, My Sweet Saviour,' whispered Belle, 'help me.' She followed because there was nothing else to do. Tray stopped, a dark wolfish shape, raising his head.

'Tray!' called May, 'Come here at once, at once, you know me!'

He put his head in the air and stalked slowly into the forest.

Belle gave up. The dream was too strong and a tide carried her on into it. The shadows sucked in the lithe brindled form of the dog, then her mother-in-law, then she herself, giving no quarter. 'Not the wood,' she said as she walked into it, hurrying to catch May's sleeve so that they might travel together for safety, and realising as she did so that for as long as she had had a brain to think with she had wanted to walk like this through the woods at night. May stood waiting for the light of the lantern.

'Can you still see him?' Belle asked, for she no longer could.

'Oh, yes!' said May.

They walked on, close as the overgrown track would allow. It forked and they took to the right and skirted a ragged edge of high banks that hung over against the sky and gave off a musty fragrance. The lantern cast a dancing glow over the under-growth. May whistled softly.

'I can't see him,' said Belle.

'I can. There.'

Sometimes the pointed head would emerge close to them, and once he ran almost to May's knee, panting with what might have been glee, like a pup playing.

In spite of the hardship to her feet and the spikes that tore at her clothes, the forest was delightful to Belle. Shafts of dusty moonlight fell through the darkness, revealing here a column of ivy, there a staggered rank of moony toadstools. We will never get out, she thought, taking another narrow trail that plucked and scratched. Never go back. She shuddered, thrilled, and it seemed to her that the forest closed behind them like a door.

'We are so far in,' she whispered to May, who did not hear.

We have been walking an age, she thought. It must get heavy, a man's head, and a big one at that. Perhaps when I get home, I will tell Hugh—and then she thought she must have slept. She had not been home for such a long time. Ellwin was not home. Home was finished. A man's head under a mantle was a terrible thing to dream about. The wood began to climb, a thin, stony track running up through a dense, pressing tangle that did its best to hinder their progress, till they emerged at a high, flat place where a faint smell of wood smoke hung on the air and a dim smudge of light glowered at the base of a high rock.

'What is it?' whispered Belle.

'He went in there.'

Belle made out a squat building. The light showed them the door.

'I don't want to go in there,' she said.

May crossed herself, ducked her head and went in without hesitation. Belle stood for only a moment before following.

She saw the body straight away and wanted to run. It was shapeless, covered by a cloak but still hideously foreshortened. It lay on what seemed a rock ledge, with its big feet sticking out comically. A crude lantern burned on the ground, and the dog stood shaking its hindquarters in the light, making up to a blinking, scowling old woman and a filthy sleeping boy stretched in the dirt. Belle thought she had never seen anything uglier than the woman, whose vile jerking lip held too much water. The woman said tonelessly, 'Lord God, protect all the righteous, Mary, Mother of God, protect us, in the name of the Lord, go!'

Realising the woman's terror, Belle could have laughed.

'I am his mother,' May said.

The boy frowned in his sleep and the old woman coughed. 'His mother,' she said. 'Tell me this. How comes this one killed? Fool knew it. Told him many a time not to go. His mother!' She spoke as if she were grumbling about the getting of a meal or the making of a fire. She was mad. The mad could speak more freely.

'What's *she*?' the old woman spat in Belle's direction.

'I have his head. Here,' said May and showed it.

Belle put her hands to her mouth and laughed, and the old woman gibbered, stretching out a claw. 'Filth!' she cried. The boy woke up and raised himself onto one elbow, blinking.

'Go!' cried the old woman, crossing herself.

The dog ran about like a fool. The boy saw the head and was wide awake, struck stupid. He drew a knife. Belle looked at it with distant fear. 'Why, where's the need for that?' she said quietly, amazed at her own voice. The boy's hand was shaking. Both of them are afraid, she thought, more afraid than we are, even though they could kill us. There must be a whole band of them nearby. Fear made her giddy.

She stepped forward, astonishing herself. 'She is his mother,' she explained. 'Surely you can see it in their faces. Don't ask me how, but she is. She wants him buried whole and she wants to take her leave, that is all, and then we will go—' But of course she realised as she said it that they could never find the way home.

'His mother is dead!' the old woman said.

'No,' said May.

'His mother is dead!'

'No.'

'Who's with you?' the boy croaked.

'No-one!'

'How do I know?' His voice was slightly pleading.

'Dame Lane,' May said, and smiled.

Everyone looked at her. The old woman crossed herself again.

'Dame Lane,' said May, 'of course it is you. I have known you for years. I know all of you. I don't care what you do and I don't care what happens to us, her or myself or any of you. But I am sure that I am going to kiss my son goodbye. Then I will go. You may do as you please, but I can promise you this: if any try to hinder our going, I will call with my last breath on Bayardine to avenge me, dead as he is.'

'Fool dog!' said Dame Lane. 'Down! Take your foul breath away!'

'Do it,' said the boy, gesturing with the tip of the knife. 'Quickly! Say your goodbyes then for God's sake, go!'

Belle laughed, unable to help it. Tears came to her eyes. 'We cannot *get* home,' she said.

'You got here,' he said rudely. He was trembling.

'I can't see the likeness,' Dame Lane said.

Belle laughed again.

'You are bold!' the old woman snapped.

Thin and leisurely as snail tracks, a few dark trails had crept down the grey rock from the body, and a little pool of blood had gathered below. May went to the body and raised the hood of the cloak, her back to them, bowed over. There was no sound. The tip of the boy's knife pointed to the ground.

'There, my dear,' said May, 'there, my dear, my poor little dear, all one now!'

After some minutes she lifted her head and arranged the body to her liking, with the shirt she had made covering all, then turned away, folding her hands before her like a nun. Belle saw that the body looked even worse, for May had placed the head clumsily or it had rolled a little, putting the whole humpish thing out of harmony. The hound, upon its belly, stretched its head and put out a long pink tongue, lapping delicately at the little pool of blood.

May held out her hand. 'Come, we'll go,' she said.

'Go?' said Belle, 'Go where? We'll never find the way.' She remembered her waiting bed, the parrot in the cage, and all her life seemed like something used and laid away.

'How's she got it then? His head?' The old woman sucked in her lips very far and spat them out again. 'Hey? Who did it? You tell me that! Come through her, all of it. Mark me.'

'Sh!' said the boy.

'You are right,' said May. 'All of it through me. My husband, Harlock, killed him because he thought he was my sweetheart. As if anyone could! Tell them all. If any want to take revenge, let them. I'll make it easy for them.' She stooped her head to go through the door.

'I don't like it. It's too strange,' the boy grumbled.

'It is wicked!' said the old woman.

May stepped out and Belle followed. She awoke from a dream. The moon was very high above, and the treetops whispered against a pale sky. They stood looking at one another.

'Down there,' said Belle, swallowing, all her fear returning. 'Let's get away from this place quickly.' But before they had begun to pick their way back down the stony track the boy had emerged behind them, his knife sheathed. 'Hoy!' he called. They turned, wary.

'You'll not get out of here if you don't know the way,' he said rudely. 'Christ knows how you got here but you'll not get out. Wait and I'll put you on the path. Where is it you're going?'

'To Ellwin Hall,' said May.

'Ellwin,' he repeated thoughtfully. His lip hung loose. 'Wait. A word with the old one.' He retreated and re-emerged a moment later to lead the way.

'Is she not afraid to be left alone?' Belle asked.

'She's watched with many a corpse,' the boy said flatly, not looking back. 'This won't be her last. She's not afraid. Poor Bayardine won't do her no harm. Know what she said when I told her you come from Ellwin? Ellwin Hall? she says. Who'd have thought he had such blood in him? He shat and stank like all the rest, God love him.'

He did not speak again and they walked on in silence.

Burnet awoke with a start in the stifling darkness. He thought he had only slept for a few minutes or so since he'd lain down hours ago, but the fire was out and he had not seen it die. He'd been crying all night. Bayardine was dead and the hound gone, and the emptiness of the hut weighed upon him like a stone.

He had not undressed. His hand was on the hilt of his knife. He thought of the man he'd seen, the face that had grown stern and looked away from his own death, the figure by the beck with its bow carried lightly. The mystery tormented him. Why, what have any of us done that he should want to kill us all? Did I do him some terrible wrong? Did Bayardine?

His fear was intense. How could there ever be safety now? The man hid behind every tree, wanting his death. Would he hack his head off too, like that foul mess on the side of the beck, the thing they'd found when he led them to the spot? The awful moment of silence that had come upon them, those rough brown men, each one feeling his own death like a breath at the ear. Bayardine. Only when he saw the thing's bitten nails did he believe it.

He cried freely and wetly into the darkness, then got up and stumbled over the step into the bright night. He would not sleep again tonight, he knew, so he went back for his old coat and walked up and down in the clearing between the huts, unable to be still. I'd rather be killed out here, he thought, than stabbed in the dark in there; he wouldn't even see where he was aiming. Burnet shook his limbs and his shoulders. His knife was at hand. No-one could get through, he thought, they'd never get in here. But it was too late—the sanctuary felt breached.

He passed the pile of wood that Bayardine had stacked earlier. When? He could not remember. After all, only another dead man. What's one more in a world like this? He'd seen dead men before, but never one murdered. He looked about. It was the kind of place where one met murder, indeed. The place enfolded him. This morning he had eaten hot broth. The smell and the taste of it came back and was also the place, as was the memory of the women singing together, or the cold morning voice of the forest, and the way he felt his skin had grown another layer so that now he no longer felt the cold so acutely.

He supposed he would live out his life here. For some reason, the realisation did not fill him with horror. If this is to be it, the thought came, then it is mine, and it is breached—almost—and he was angry and no longer so afraid. He stalked about the settlement feeling his brain grow clear and bright as ice. How could they all sleep? Or did they? Death had tired them. Bayardine, the best thief, gone. Damned if I don't go and see him, he thought then. Why should I be afraid of him, head or no head, did he ever harm me? No. Why shouldn't I sit with him awhile? Poor Bayard, up there with only Dame Lane for company—and Rawl, asleep by now, no doubt. And wasn't I his best friend?

He had not wanted to sit with Bayardine, but now he couldn't sleep. He rubbed his eyes and blew his nose, then walked quickly away towards the southern rampart. A sleepy guard watched him pass, raising a hand. He stood outside. If I am to spend my life there, he thought, it cannot be as a prison. Might as well be dead. He was careless, Bayardine. Not me. These are my ferns, I can walk in them if I like.

He walked on for a while. I go as silent as any, he thought, pleased. A smile came to his face.

He thought he heard a woman's voice and froze.

It wasn't Dame Lane's croak. There was nothing now. Then he heard very faintly a rustling in the leaves somewhere above, and a stone rattled. He saw a light and crouched low. They came down from the track leading up to the anchoress's old cell, passing fairly close to where he hid. Rawl went ahead without a light, two women followed, the second carrying a lantern which gave off a useless glow. He saw her face quite clearly.

'Belle,' he would have said. He knew her. The antler was in his pocket. She passed on, turning her back and hiding the light.

He stood up. He was filled more with dread than anything else. He'd grown used to a world where everyone knew more than he did, had a sense that he had not; to understand nothing was his daily fare. But this went far beyond that. Were they spirits, all these people, women walking about in the night, murderers—what had they to do with him? The hairs along his spine rose like hackles, and he followed.

He shook with something, maybe anger. Why should he not understand? Who was she? *She* knew all about *him,* he was sure, and he wanted to run, catch her arm, read her face when she recognised him. She would, of course. She had all the answers. But he did not run. One thing he knew. She was dangerous, she had always been dangerous. He must bide his time. Bayardine was lured with a woman. I am very good at this, he thought, smiling as he kept them silent company, good ghost that he was. And his blood rose, anticipating adventure.

O ne torch smoked, one great log burned slowly on the fire. Harlock needed company that night. The men of the household, ordered to make merry and forbidden by custom to retire, had long ago expired and slumped where they were, drunk and snoring. Some sprawled across the dismantled trestles, some on the soaked rushes with the dogs. Liquor dripped slowly from an overturned cup and a dog's leg twitched, outstretched. The place stank of stale beer and wine

Hugh and Harlock could not sleep and they'd drunk so much that more made no difference.

'What was I to think?' Harlock said again, addressing his cup in exasperation. 'What would anyone think?' Some time after midnight, before the claret had run out, he had found himself confiding the truth of it all to Hugh Rennock in a befuddled way, and now thought: Was I mad? To tell him? He has not shown understanding. His manner grows insolent.

'Seeing the two so close, I naturally thought—' His hand suddenly flopped like a separate creature and the cup jumped, slopping some of its load. He looked at it.

'Yes,' said Hugh, irritated, his eyes sleep-starved. 'You've said that.' The old fool! he thought. Kill me an outlaw, he says. Yes, sir, without more ado! The man was mad. He grimaced and forced more wine into the queasy bag of his stomach. He wanted no part in a family quarrel. Mad, the lot of them. He'd put his sister into a snake pit. 'Gah!' he spat, grinning with his gums. 'Gah!'

'It was your arrow,' Harlock said.

'Well?' Disgust sat about Hugh like a collar. I'll not bow to him again, he thought bitterly. Two men now. Two men of no account. A dirty business, this last. 'You can't push it on to me,' he said. 'Kill an outlaw, you said. How can I help it if it turns out to be your wife's spawn? Not likely, is it?'

'Spawn? My wife's!' Harlock was not sure why he felt so suddenly furious at this word. It was like thrown muck. He leaned forward slowly, with the steadiness of the absolutely drunk. 'You forget yourself,' he said quietly, reaching for his cup and missing, groping for it with a shaking hand. 'Remember who I am.'

Hugh did not speak.

Harlock laughed. 'There is a stench in here,' he said.

'Your wife's spawn,' said Hugh, unable to help himself.

Harlock jumped to his feet slowly, reaching for his sword and Hugh half rose, drawing his knife with the lovely bone handle like two fishes. Their backs were smooth in his hand. A strange, doltish fatigue sat upon their anger.

'Agh!' said Harlock, sitting again and sweeping the air with one arm to show that he would not play. Hugh stood looking with distaste at the tip of the knife, where a string of dried blood still clung.

'You didn't clean it properly,' he said, outraged.

Harlock sucked air into the piercing hollow of his tooth and winced. 'The curse of hell on these teeth of mine!' he cried peevishly.

'You didn't clean it.'

The other men champed like animals in their sleep.

'Well?' said Harlock. 'You clean it.'

Hugh quite unaccountably wanted to cry because of the string of blood on his knife.

'I didn't dirty it,' he said defiantly. 'I don't want to clean it. I don't want it.'

'Give it back then.'

'No!'

Hugh sheathed it, dirty as it was. The great room heaved about him and the knife wanted to be used. Harlock brought up a splash of wine that stained his stomacher, and it made them both laugh, gazing at each other like old friends till the laugh was spent and they were cold again, and the shadows had advanced further from the four corners of the hall.

Hugh stood jerkily and walked about. There had been a hawk, he remembered. It seemed like a bad omen.

'What was I to think?' Harlock said again.

'Ah, it was not your fault,' said Hugh.

'Nay, of course not.'

'You said yourself, what would any man think? One doesn't expect one's wives to have sons.'

'Nay, of course not. If she had told me— She should have told me. How am I to know if I am not told?'

'Aye.'

Phoebe, he thought. My Phoebe.

There was a sound from the corner of the room. Both of them jumped.

'A mouse,' said Harlock.

Hugh was breathless. Christ, do not, please do not let me think of spirits, he prayed. His tongue felt thick.

'Ha ha,' said Harlock, 'frightened by a mouse.'

But Hugh felt there was nowhere in the hall where he could sit and be free from this creeping at his back. Harlock looked at him as if he saw something over his shoulder. 'He's come to see her,' Harlock said, smiling thinly, though his eyes wore a look of permanent shock. 'Walking about the house without his head.'

'Quiet!'

'Wants it back.' A smothered laugh escaped.

The carrion work fast, Hugh thought. What will he be like by morning?

Harlock poured more wine for them both, then drank like a thirsty child. 'She should have told me,' he said, upending the flagon. 'Where's Sim?' He went to the door and threw it open and called.

'Sim!' His voice echoed on stone.

'We'll see the dawn in,' he said, returning. 'What damned o'clock is it? Feels like the dead hour.' He prodded a snoring heap with his toe. 'What, are they all dead? Fine company! Sim! Sim! Afraid, the sneaking, simpering little—'

A nervous servant, one of the very few not drunk, appeared in the doorway.

'Where's Sim?'

'My lord,' the man said, advancing pale and bleary, 'Sim has gone.'

'Gone?'

'Gone, my lord. His clothes . . . everything.' He spoke apologetically, swaying slightly from weariness.

For a moment Harlock was silent. He thought of Sim alone on some road in the middle of this dreary night, and wondered where he would go. He'd never come back.

Gone to join the rabble.

'Bring us some wine,' said Harlock.

Much later, having fallen into restless silence, Harlock began to weep softly. Great tears soaked his ruddy cheeks. 'Tooth hurts,' he said.

Hugh was still awake, paralysed, watching a flea feed upon a vein in the back of his hand. He twitched with annoyance. He must go to bed. He must walk through the house and lie alone watching a candle flicker till morning brought that tired light that meant he could sleep.

Harlock slid to the floor as if his bones had melted.

A long time later, there were footsteps, and Hugh lifted his head to listen. Too brisk, he decided, for a ghost. Then William appeared with two servants at his back and stood on the edge of the room like a swimmer on the brink of a water of uncertain depth. His clothes had been hastily thrown on and his hair stood up, more when he passed his hand through it and licked his pale pendant lips, his eyes flickering over the scene. He had grace of a kind, Hugh thought as the boy came forward, pausing to look aside at the sleepers.

'Shall we rouse them, sir?' one of the servants asked.

He seemed surprised at the question and frowned for a moment. 'No,' he said, unsure, 'no, no—leave them, I suppose,' and came to stand over his father.

'Father!' he started strongly, but his voice gave out at first try.

Harlock lay sleeping with a scowl of pain on his face.

'Father! Sim's gone.' His hair got in his face, greasy. Tears came to his eyes. 'He's gone! What did you do? What did you do? I've seen Belle. She told me terrible things. What's happening? What's happening?'

Hugh laughed. 'You and my sister,' he said insultingly, then, 'What does Belle know? You must not believe everything that Belle tells you. She is my sister, you know.'

William looked at him blankly.

Harlock began to wake, to twitch about and swallow and sneer, his eyes still closed. He rose a little from the floor but subsided again with a groan.

'Father,' said William wearily. His eyes were red. 'You have spoiled everything.'

Harlock began to cry.

William stood back, perplexed. He had to give some orders. He waited, biting his lip.

'What have I done?' said Harlock, his eyes still closed. 'My tooth! Killed a damned outlaw, that is all.'

'My brother,' said William in a loud voice. 'She said he was my brother. Everyone knows. *Everyone knows.*' He looked about with wild eyes. I will not keep my voice down. Everyone knows. They're all looking to me for orders.

'William!' Harlock said.

William stooped over him. Harlock put out a hand and grasped his son's arm. 'You will not be half the man that I am,' he said, and William jerked up, away from him, so strongly that a piece of his shirt caught on Harlock's big jade ring and was ripped.

'Oh God and Damnation and Hell!' cried Harlock. William flinched. *'I cannot stand this pain.'*

'Have his tooth pulled,' said William, suddenly sure of what to do. He drew a breath that lifted his chin. 'Attend to his needs then put him to bed.' He turned to Hugh Rennock while the servants were lifting his father between them. 'Rennock,' he said, 'you will leave this house tomorrow.' Then he left, marching smartly through the door and beginning to smile faintly as he crossed the wide passage and mounted the stairs. I did that well, he thought. His spaniel pup came to meet him at the head of the stairs and flopped along beside him to his mother's room. When I have charge, he thought, I will change things.

The curtains were closed about the bed.

'Mother,' he called softly.

After a pause, her voice said, tired, 'Draw the curtains, dear.'

When he saw his mother he knew that everything was true. She said nothing but smiled at him ruefully, a little embarrassed, shrugging her shoulders.

'It's all right,' he said. 'Everything will be all right now. I'm seeing to things.'

She reached out and touched the tear in his shirt. 'What's this?' she asked.

'Nothing,' he said, looking down.

'I'll mend it for you later,' she said, closing her eyes.

urnet was quite sure he'd never seen this house before. It called forth nothing, answered no questions. He wished he'd done something now, made himself known, but like a fool he had watched the two women go on alone from the forest's edge, following skilfully, till now the house had swallowed them up. It stood like a beast with a gaping mouth, facing the forest, absolutely silent, elevated and surrounded by pastures.

How could he know her if she lived in there? It was impossible. Burnet looked up at the sky. There was time. For what? To stand about and freeze and think of his uselessness, always to watch and see and never to take a part. Or go home and try to sleep, and wake a thousand times and think: Bayardine is dead, and: She was there and I never asked her. Who am I? Suppose she hates me? Suppose she had me killed? Why? She would not! No.

He could get in anywhere, given time, and he could get in there but he'd never find her. If they caught him, they'd kill him. His blood tingled. Go back there and lie in my hut, he thought. Or what? Walk about the house opening doors? Here I am! But I'll not go home till morning. What could happen? Any window's an escape. And if I find nothing, well—I'll learn to know the house, and then—and if she's not alone? Abed with her husband! Husband? Did she? Surely not. And what if she is, I'll never find her anyway, and if I do she'll scream for help and they'll take me away and hang me up in a tree and I'll die.

Still, he walked out from the sheltering trees, between the outbuildings and up to the high arch, where he stood for a while in the blackness under the wall looking at the stone creatures carved above, an eagle and a lion and two rampant unicorns, whose wedge-like hoofs formed the zenith. He could be so quiet he doubted his own existence sometimes. He moved forward, stealing, feeling like an animal. The gate was unlocked. He stiffened. This was unnatural, horribly inviting. The women were distraught, he thought, they have forgotten to lock it. But surely someone watched in a house like this. After an age of listening he carefully pushed against it and felt it give, waited again then got it open just enough to slide his body into the gap and through, and so passed under the arch and stood looking out upon a dim courtyard. His eyes counted doors and darkened windows, measured the distance from where he stood to a corresponding arch on the far side. Looking up he saw the chimneys against a bright sky. He remembered everything that Bayardine had taught him. Wait. Be patient. You have all the time you will ever need.

He skirted the yard slowly and came to a heavy door that opened by means of a thick metal ring formed like a rope. Two hands would be needed to turn it silently. Hardly worth the try, for this could not also be—

It was unlocked. This time his brow turned cold. No great house should lie unguarded like this. He imagined darkness and spitting hell on the other side of the door. So he waited a while for his heart to slow down again, but it did not and he had to carry on with it shaking him from within. The heavy ring was in his hands. It would toll like a summoning bell if he should drop it, as some devil urged him to do, but his will resisted. A sense of dreaming came over him. He lifted the ring and opened the door no more than a crack, thanking God that the hinges were well greased. And then he waited.

Nothing happened. He continued on around the courtyard walls. Twice he made the round of it, then slipped under the second arch and down a pitchy passage that emerged on a wide terrace that ran the length of the house. A flight of steps went down to a lawn. Burnet began to enjoy himself. He haunted the gardens and the outer walls thoroughly, saw a gloomy light shining from a rank of tall windows set high in the side of the house, a dead light that did not worry him much. He heard no sounds.

At last he returned to the open door, drew his knife and went in. The dream intensified. He stood in a stone hall with the ceiling very far away and a staircase ascending, the moon coming in at a window. Some distance ahead and to his left a door stood open. The dead glow came from there. He could smell the sweet smell of the dying fire, and he stole across to the door and looked in and saw at once why he had gone unchallenged. God is helping me, he thought. He saw riches, hangings, sleeping men, vomit, fallen flagons, cups. Not a dog stirred.

Burnet smiled. Was I ever as good at anything as I am at this, he thought, and crushed the desire to pick all their pockets, take the collars from the dogs and the rings from their fingers. But he would take no chances. He looked about himself. Inch by inch, he would learn the house. First this floor, the kitchen and the buttery and counting house. Then, when he was ready, he'd go up.

His eyes moved to the stairs, rising gracefully to a point where they turned, each tread so worn that a gentle ripple seemed to pass through the whole. I am asleep, he thought. I am under water. I am dead. And I am not afraid.

i want to be home, Hugh thought, going to Belle's room, I want to be home now, this second, none of this has happened. He blinked angrily. It was not Caddenhope *now* that he wanted, but Caddenhope as it was, Belle as she was, his father alive and he himself in his youth and strength, climbing to the saddle while she watched him with some pride. Before all this. His brain felt damp and tired. Before what? Why, what really had happened? Nothing. He could not remember. Surely, nothing so bad that this sense of dread should sit so heavily upon him, tingling to the ends of his fingers and toes. He was not a bad man. If he could just explain it to her she would understand.

'Who's there?' she said sharply when he knocked on the door.

'Hugh.'

There was a long silence.

'Open the door,' he called.

He heard a silky rustling. 'Go away,' she said, close at hand.

He closed his eyes, leaning his brow against the hard wood. 'I am here,' he said. 'I am not going away. Say what you will, Belle, say what you will! I've come to hear it, God damn me, I'm not going away.'

She said nothing.

'You're cruel!' he said. 'Don't you know me yet? Treat me like a dog? Me, Belle! Open the door, it's me! This foul, rank, icy place, I hate it! There's only you that knows me. Turn me away? You can't.' There were tears behind his eyes.

She opened the door and stood looking at him with the particular look that she kept for his gravest offences. He smiled. 'What have you done?' she cried, her face furious, and pulled

❖ 161

him in and shook him till his head nodded. 'What have you done? Poor May is mad! Killing! She's had me out half the night, didn't you know? I've been in the woods, Hugh! Oh, Hugh, it was beautiful! Bayardine! Can you believe it? I can't sleep now, I can't. I feel mad. She had his head—his head—' She paced about with her long fingers locked together. 'How can I sleep now? I can't even lie down!' She started to cry.

'That was not me,' he said, going to her and trying to take her by the shoulders, but she pulled away. 'That was Harlock. I swear I had no part in the mutilation. Why should I? How could I know? Her son! Ridiculous! No-one could have known it. The man was an outlaw, the worst! You know that! This is unfair, Belle, *you* are unfair. I did not know. How many times do I have to say that? I did not know. I will not be treated like a murderer.'

A flush crept over his face as he said it.

'But I saw him.' She stood by the covered hump of the parrot's cage and stared at him with frightened eyes. 'I saw him. He was just a man. She held him like this, like a baby. You did not see!'

Bayardine, kicking and jerking. Hugh blinked rapidly. 'I saw enough,' he said quietly.

She put out her hands and grasped his arms, leaning forward to look at his face. 'Oh, Hugh!' she said, 'oh, Hugh, isn't this a terrible business?'

The tears came to his eyes. 'I broke no law,' he said. 'Harlock sickened me. I am not so bad, I—'

'Yes,' she said, 'yes,' hugged him quickly, then pushed him away and went to stand at the window. 'Dear God, it is beautiful out there,' she said.

He followed her. 'Have you forgiven me?' he asked at her shoulder.

'Look,' she said, 'the moon going down.'

'Have you forgiven me?'

'Go to chapel,' she told him harshly. 'It's not for me to forgive. Do you think I'm your confessor?' She walked away, angry again. 'Listen to yourself! You are never to blame! An outlaw? A mother's son! For what? For Harlock! For sport! Go away, Hugh, go away, please.'

'Go away?' He laughed. 'I am *ordered* away. By your husband. Your husband! Ha! I'm in disgrace. Follow the law and do your duty and you're in disgrace. Care for your sister's honour and you're in disgrace—'

'My honour?' She frowned. 'What are you talking about, my honour?'

'Honour? What honour?' He too was angry. 'All I did was for the best,' he said doggedly, 'everything, everything. Things aren't always what they seem. Why are you treating me like this, as if I were a stranger? Am I? Am I?' He turned with a stiff gesture that dislodged from a ledge in the wall a bowl of the fine perfumed flour she used to whiten her skin. It covered the floor and a cloud of dust hung in the air, teasing the nostrils.

'*Now* look!' She flung herself heavily down on the bed and sat there scowling, but he waved a dismissive hand at the mess and came to hang over her, one arm hooked around the bed post.

'Who am I?' he said. 'Tell me that. Tell me. Am I your brother? Didn't we grow up together?'

'What?'

'Didn't we? Didn't we?'

'You know we—'

'Then why are you behaving like this?' he cried. 'What have I done? What have I ever done? Nothing to harm you! I am the same, the same, don't you see that? Whatever I've done, I'm the same!'

'You know what you've done,' she said. 'I say again, go to chapel if you're troubled. I'm not your confessor.'

'But I want to tell you.' He sat down beside her and tried to look into her face. 'Listen,' he said, 'listen to this. I want to tell you everything, how I did it, what I thought, everything—'

'No,' she said.

'You have no choice.'

'No.'

'Listen. First of all you must know that—'

'*No!*' She stood up, jumping away and facing him. 'I don't want to hear! Go away! Leave me alone or I'll run away! I'll—' She looked around, putting her hands to her ears, and cried again. 'Go away! Please, go away!'

His eyes went dull.

She ran to him and began pulling and pushing at him. 'Get up,' she panted. 'Get up and go now. Please. If you want to please me, that's what you have to do. Get up, get up, get up!'

He stood so suddenly that she fell over.

'Poor Belle,' he said, brushing down his sleeves. She sat up, her cheeks red and wet, looking at him with wounded eyes.

'When all this is over—' she said.

He walked to the window, raising dust with every step, looking vainly for dawn. The parrot under its cover made a sound like a clicking tongue, and he lifted the corner of the cloth and saw the creature sitting there, patient as a statue. The parrot was older than his memory and had belonged first to his mother and then to Belle. In the gloom he made out its round eye watching him benignly, and he stared back.

'Will you please go,' she said quietly. 'I am tired.'

He dropped the cloth and turned. For a moment they looked at one another.

'Thank you for your kindness,' he said stiffly, and walked out of the room. After a moment he heard her fasten the door behind him. Though he wanted to break it down, he walked away. He hated her. He wanted company. At the top of the stairs he stopped, half turned and stood irresolute, but only for a second before continuing on his way.

Where? he thought. Where? Alone, above, to think of Bayardine coming for his head. He shivered. This dark, filthy place! Wake up some good man and play cards.

Down he went.

At the turn of the stair, where a faltering torch cast moving shadows, he stopped. First the hairs on the nape of his neck rose up, then he saw the man ascending towards him in the thin dark, a long knife in his hand. Dread engulfed him. The man stopped too, looking up, his face unclear. Then the flame leapt and Hugh's heart stopped.

John Heron. Dead John Heron.

Hugh thought that he screamed but no sound came out. Silence rolled down the walls and a terrible sinking sickness, a fear like death or madness, crippled him. How long he stood paralysed he did not know.

At some point he turned and ran. He could not breathe. At Belle's door he beat upon the panels, face turned towards the obscure shadows of the stairhead where the ghost would appear. His useless mouth gaped, unable to cry, and in the brightness of the moonlight falling in through the tall window at the end of the passage, he felt exposed and naked.

She did not come.

Hugh hurled himself at the door with a strangled cry. It opened and he fell in. 'Lord God—' her scared face said as he fumbled with the lock. His fingers would not work.

'What?' she said, as if he'd spoken.

'Lock it.' His voice failed. 'Lock it. Lock it! *Lock the damned thing!*'

Frightened, she obeyed, then watched amazed as he stumbled to her bed and crawled upon it into the corner, where he turned and crouched, trembling and staring fixedly at the door.

She went to him. 'What is it?' she whispered. 'Hugh! Don't frighten me! What is it?'

'Sh!' His violence shocked her.

She followed his gaze, listening. There was no sound but his breathing. 'Oh, look at you!' she said. 'Look at you! Oh, Hugh! It's one of your nightmares, that's all. No wonder.' And she crawled up beside him and put her arms around him.

He could not bear it. 'He's coming,' he whispered. 'I killed him, I killed him, Belle, but he's coming.'

'No,' she said. 'No.'

'Yes! On the stairs. I saw him. With a knife. I cut his throat, now he wants to cut mine.'

'No, you didn't. You haven't slept. That's all, that's all.'

Hugh groaned. 'It's too late to pray!' he said.

Belle stood up. 'Shall I look?' she asked kindly.

'No! Sh!' He raised his head to listen. 'What was that?'

'I didn't hear anything.' She went to the door and stooped there, listening, then turned and smiled at him. 'Nothing.' The smile remained and she looked about her, yawning. 'Now I am very tired,' she said, and came towards him and sat down, looking at him steadily and covering his hands. 'I feel I'm in a dream. You too. Listen to me. There's nothing out there, noth- ing at all but your guilty conscience, do you understand me? Bayardine's gone.'

Hugh looked at her blankly for a moment then began to laugh.

She drew away from him, disturbed.

'Bayardine!' he said as if it were a great joke. 'Ah yes, Bayar- dine!'

'Don't,' she said. 'Now you really make me afraid. Don't. You will go mad, Hugh, you must sleep.' She frowned. 'You make no sense. Lie down here, if you will, and go to sleep.'

He was not laughing now. She went cold. It was something

in the way his head thrust forward and his eyes watched her with sudden steady interest. 'Belle,' he said, 'Belle.'

'What?' she said softly.

'Belle,' he said again.

Something stronger than his fear had taken hold of him.

'Oh, God,' she said, sensing danger.

'Belle,' said Hugh, 'it wasn't Bayardine I saw. Now I'm going to tell you, Belle, because you will forgive me because you cannot help yourself because I am your brother, and if you forgive me I can be saved.'

His eyes, she thought. Poor Hugh.

'John Heron,' he said. 'I killed John Heron. I took him into the forest and cut his throat, and then I finished him off with a rock. I swear it, I swear—'

Nothing happened in her face. Then she looked aside and he saw a faint flicker in her eyes, as if she'd just remembered something sad that had happened a long time ago.

'It was for you,' he said.

'For me?' she repeated.

He could have screamed. What have I done? What have I done? The world falls down. Unable to bear her stillness, he stood up and walked about in the perfumed mess on the floor. 'For you,' he said, 'for you, all for you. Do you think I kill for nothing? What am I? Mad? Your brother, your brother, Belle! What do you say? What do you say? Eh?'

She said nothing.

'Some things cannot be allowed to happen. You see that.' Hugh would not stand near the door. Spirits have a way of passing through nine-foot walls. Not long now till dawn, surely not long. She must come back to Caddenhope with him, the nights there were also very long. He pulled a lump of skin from the root of his thumbnail and a pain shot through his palm.

Blood appeared and he studied it. 'For God's sake, speak,' he said.

Belle raised one hand to her lips as if she might be feeling a little sick. 'He is here?' she said faintly.

'You remind me! He is here, he is here, he is here!'

'No!' She said it as if it were too funny for words.

'I saw him.'

'No,' she said and put her head down for a long time.

'This is hard for you,' he said. His teeth were chattering. 'But it will be easier. It will pass, believe me, it will pass, and if I had never told you and the years had passed, there would have come a time when I could have said to you, Belle, do you remember John Heron? And you would have said, Who? John Who? Why did I tell you, then? Why?' He laughed. 'Oh God, what a fool I am!'

She looked up. 'Go away,' she said, breathing very fast, and suddenly it was as if a wall surrounded her.

'He was low,' said Hugh, and a note of desperation had crept into his voice. 'The blood won't mix.' His own words conjured a picture of wounds, spilt gore running freely, flowing like streamlets into one bright river that babbled its playful way to a crimson sea. 'For you!' he said.

She jumped to her feet, leaning forward from the waist and hissing at him. 'Don't lay it at my feet! Go away! Go away, go away, go away! I can't stand to look at you!' She went as far from him as she could, backed into the wall and stared him out like a cornered sheep.

He hardened. She will stamp with her hoof now, he thought. Vain bravery. He went close and spoke very quietly. 'Because I love you,' he said. 'That is all. Understand.'

There was a silence between them, full of the past.

She smiled faintly. 'Morning soon,' she said.

Tears filled his eyes.

Then she pushed at him and he fell back. 'Now go,' she said, 'no more,' and pushed and pushed till he was at the door.

'Out there?' he whispered.

'Out there!' she said. 'And I hope it's true and I hope he slits you like a fish!' She fumbled with the lock. He watched tears dropping from the end of her chin. What matter? What matter any of it?

In the passage he drew his knife.

'See,' she said from the door, 'there is nothing.'

He looked neither backwards nor to right nor left, but walked quickly to Harlock's apartment where he found the door unfastened and Harlock snoring on the bed. The tooth was pulled.

'Listen,' said Hugh, shaking him, 'listen.'

Harlock did not wake but his mouth opened like a bloody trap, a red membrane of jellied saliva stretched between the lips.

Hugh kicked the bed in frustration. 'Company,' he muttered, 'for Christ's sweet sake, company.'

Harlock jerked and gurgled, subsiding then into deep, distant sleep where his thoughts pricked him like bee stings and showed in his aggravated face.

'Listen,' said Hugh, crouching and speaking quietly into the waxy darkness of Harlock's ear. 'It was all for nothing. Cut the throat and throw him away, still he comes back. Cut off the head, the body still walks. I tell you, we are not safe, man. Not just your outlaw and my ploughboy—we could kill them all, kill and kill and kill the whole ugly rabble of them. What then? Can you see them? An army of filth facing us down.' He groaned. 'Oh God, it's horrible! What shall we do to slay them now? Hack them all to gobbets and they'll come back! Hands and noses, arms and legs, spleen and liver and all, writhing about like grubs under a stone and getting back together, sticking fast, walking and grinning and getting their knives and coming back for us and—oh, sweet Jesus, it is not over, it is not over, it will never be over.'

He could have rested his head and slept but he dared not close his eyes. Harlock snored on. I cannot be here, thought Hugh. I cannot be anywhere. Company, company. Where can I go? Where's morning? Surely no night was ever this long, surely— never a sound, never a cock—blessed things all dead, throats all wrung by ghostly hands. There is no more morning and this is Hell, this endless night.

He listened. The only sound in the house was the troubled breathing of the man on the bed. From one second to the next his fear boiled over like milk left too long on the fire, and he seized Harlock's candle and burst from the room, met an empty channel of darkness that sprang alight to his candle's glow, rocking crazily as he dashed its length to the servants' staircase. His knees were weak, his bowels watered. Coming to the hall once more, he sat down in the company of those few drunk fellows who still remained sleeping by the spent and whispering fire, which he poked and coaxed until one or two tiny flames stirred helpfully. I'm ill, he thought, shivering. The door stood open at the end of the hall. He feared the space beyond, but feared more the walk from here to there to close it.

'Friends,' he said hopefully, 'will you not wake up?'

They slept on as if enchanted. Perhaps they are, he thought.

'A song?' he said, and laughed, then lay on his back amongst the comforting warmth of the bony hounds, looking up at the roof-tree with his knife still in his hand. And it was true, the night was endless.

Poor John. Poor, poor John.

He sat in the shelter blowing on his frozen fingers. The crows covered the corn. With a start, he leapt to his feet and seized the clapper, shaking it with a desperate fury that set it beating and beating till the flock rose up like a great black cloud, killing the sun.

Burnet awoke, shocked. Surely he'd not slept? What had he

missed? He cursed himself, sweating, finding himself in a nest, the knife still by him. Then he remembered:

How his heart had quickened as soon as he'd heard the footsteps, too late to run now, and then the man had appeared and stopped and stared, and he'd thought he would die of fright. It seemed to him that he'd always known in some secret part of himself that this meeting must take place, as if a seed had been planted before he was born and this was the ripening. He knew now that this man was not human, for he was everywhere, without and within, and he killed for no reason. And he knew that he could not hope to escape but must kill or be killed himself, and the knowledge shrivelled him.

Still the madness heightened: the fiend had not behaved as a fiend should, but blanched and opened its mouth without a sound, biting the air, the eyes growing wide with horror, as if weak, stupid Burnet were the Devil himself and the fiend some poor mortal. Then it had fled. Burnet heard the panic of footsteps, some commotion above, then nothing.

For a long time he'd stood bewildered on the stairs. He's playing with me, he thought and his knees shook. He thought he'd wandered into some house of air, that the woman he sought and the man he'd seen were spirits, players in some riddling game he was compelled to solve. Why were they under one roof? Kill, he thought. To kill. What chance against his knife? The air itself was sticky with fear. If he should run away, dive into the forest and pull the leaves down over him and stay very still forever, perhaps he might escape. But something deeper told him no.

So, very carefully, he had mounted the stairs. At the curve he'd smelt a perfume that tugged at his memory, paused and sniffed. There was no sense to be made of it so he'd moved on, reaching the top and finding himself at the mouth of a passage with a long window at one end. Faint white footsteps ended at a door half way down. He had stooped and discovered them to consist of a fine perfumed dust, raised his head and considered, suddenly, unaccountably calm. The world was mad and he trusted nothing. So be it. He would not go in there. A large basket sat beneath the window, large enough to hide him. So he had climbed in and sunk down, enjoying the strangeness of sheets, soiled as they were. Sooner or later, the door must open and his enemy would appear. Then one of them would die.

At the creaking of the door he peered warily over the lip of the basket. The thin dark figure stood in the passage. He is weakened, thought Burnet, somehow he is weakened, and he dared to hope for life. But the man drew a knife, a long, thin, double-edged blade that gleamed in the light from the open door, and Burnet felt a little death within.

'See,' said a woman's voice, 'there is nothing.'

And that was she. She had the answers. He knew the voice and he knew the perfume of the dust. A great weight rolled from him, like the sudden lifting of a pain. Blood? he thought. Killing? And it was all laughable. Her door closed. The murderer walked away. After him, Burnet thought weakly, but he sheathed his knife. The footsteps faded.

Soon it would be day. For a little while he lay back with closed eyes, gathering his scrambled senses. Then he rose from the basket and ran silently to her door. This one last thing, and then he would be gone.

She took the cover from the cage.

'Hello, my pretty pretty,' she whispered. 'Do you love me, then?'

The parrot looked back. Belle tried to smile but her

mouth felt stiff. 'Come kiss me then,' she said, 'come kiss me.'

She opened the door of the cage and put in her hand and stroked the soft green breast. It was warm and a small heart beat there. There was a tap at the door. Go away, Hugh, she thought, I can't bear to look at you. I loved my brother. Where has he gone? All alone to Hell. And John Heron dead. She was numb with fear of a grief she could scarcely yet feel, though it waited all around her as the knowledge of death waits round the condemned.

'I wonder if I will live,' she said softly to the parrot. It blinked.

He tapped again. 'Go away,' she whispered. She remembered the moonlit shafts in the forest and the delight of them saddened her. The idiot walls knew nothing. How lonely he will be, she thought. Poor Hugh.

Her mind was tired. Pictures arose in it. John Heron leaned across the neck of an ox, smiling at her. 'You should have seen him,' she said, smiling too. 'He was so pretty. He thought well of himself, poor thing. Do you love me, then? Do you?'

He tapped again.

Here it came, grief blossoming, not like a torrent or a veil, but like the gnawing of a small animal at the red meat of her heart. The birds are singing, she thought, surprised. It must be near dawn.

He tapped again. She turned in sudden anger and ran to the door and threw it open. John Heron stood there, so real and so impossible that she knew he was a ghost, called up by her grief. The world dimmed and returned, and still he stood there. She felt light, as if she might come loose and float. He'd changed. His eyes had grown large, aged and harrowed in his ravaged face, and a thick rust-coloured welt adorned his throat. I did not know I had forgotten his face, she thought, and didn't even know it.

She moved slowly back into her room, as slowly as he advanced. There was no greeting, no smiling. She came up against the bed and stopped, and he stopped too at some distance. And there they were, frozen like figures in a picture.

Is he dead? she thought. No.

But she'd heard of such things. Oh, poor ghost, poor ghost. Why doesn't he speak? It was terrible to die as young and foolish as he was. His eyes were strange, constant, very bright.

'Are you alive?' she whispered.

He smiled. Yes, he nodded.

Impossible.

She put her hands over her mouth and laughed till tears came out of her eyes. His eyes filled too though the smile stayed, and he opened his arms, palms upwards, raising his shoulders in a hopeless, helpless, questioning gesture.

'You cannot speak?' she said.

He shook his head.

'Oh, poor John, poor John!' She stepped towards him but stopped, shaking her head and turning away distractedly. 'What now?' she said. 'What now?'

He shook his head, then searched his clothing and at last stretched out his palm towards her. On it lay a silver antler with a ruby at the tip, part of her mother's brooch. His crude palm was grimed with dirt, a scar on the mount of Venus.

She laughed. 'I have the rest!' she cried with reckless gaiety, dashing to the bed where her cloak lay rumpled, the brooch pinned at its neck. 'Here! Look!'

But the look on his face shocked her then, for it was full of awe and a kind of dread as he gazed at the delicate head of the stag, and he faltered and drooped and sank to the floor, covering his face and bowing his shoulders. The silence of it all frightened her. She stood, looking about stupidly as if for help from the walls. One day she would wake up. Where was dawn? Yes, there they were still, the birds sleepily singing. She had only to think of them and they were there.

He looked up at her. When she saw the desperation in his eyes she fell down on one knee a little way from him, wanting to touch but afraid. Corpse-cold, she thought. Deceiving. His mouth foul, full of dead vapour and the reek of clay.

'Can I touch you?' she asked.

He held out his hands and she took them, folding the antler inside. They were cold, but living-cold. He opened them again and plucked the antler from his palm, stowing it away once more. A tiny spot of blood appeared there. Belle examined his palms as if she were going to read his future. He was alive. He smelt of dew and wood smoke. She remembered the barn in the Sallow Meadow and how he was forbidden, utterly forbidden, and she didn't care at all. She laughed again and felt his arms and shoulders and the scar of his throat. He drew back at this, smiling to show he was not offended.

A cock crowed distantly.

She leaned forward and kissed him on the mouth, which also was alive, warm and soft and sweet. And even if he were dead, she thought, I don't care. They drew apart. The sky at the window was lightening. 'What now?' she said again. 'What now?'

For a moment they sat looking at each other, dazed by the imminence of morning. Then he leaned forward and took her shoulders and gripped them hard, staring into her face with some urgency he could not speak, and jumped up and went to the door and looked out. She stood. He came back, agitated, turned around, looked at the window, turned back to her hopelessly. A little chill crept through her. After all, she thought, what is this place? Certainly not my home.

There was no time to think.

'I'll come,' she said. Her voice had dried up and it came out small.

She saw gratitude in his face, and fear, and many other things. Her own fear made all things clear. She felt it inside, like a child in the belly. Now, she thought, now, this very second. I am walking out of my life. When she moved, she moved through fear, and it was like walking through deep water. She took her cloak from the bed, put it on and walked out of her life.

he feet of mice ran whisperingly about the hidden recesses of the hall. The fire made small reassuring noises.

'There is nothing enduring,' said Hugh.

When I was a boy, he thought, I loved this time, rising in the dark and dressing for the hunt, the sun coming up as I rode out with the cold in my nostrils, the blood heating at the sound of the horns, and then the lovely shrilling of the hounds.

There was a sensation in his breast of a gentle, lilting fall, utterly and exquisitely sad. Beyond the door a twilight cavern lay. A picture was now just discernible on its far wall, only the paler details visible—the squared knees of a rearing steed, a fluttering pennant, flowers that starred the darkness. Hugh strained his eyes on these, then yawned till thin tears appeared on his face. When he opened his eyes, the world blurred and cleared suddenly, showing him a man and a woman, dark-clothed and hooded, passing under the hooves of the steed as they crossed the space between the stairfoot and the heavy outer door.

They were gone. He blinked.

He knew, beyond all possibility of doubt, what he had seen. His bones clenched. The dead come for the quick.

Hugh lurched from his place, his mouth falling open on a cry that stuck in his throat, then fell to his knees in the muck, wide awake, palms prickling, a pain in his chest. She'd be gone forever once dawn was up. He climbed up, holding on to the trestle, staggered to the door with his limbs as heavy as lead. I cannot stand it, he thought, cannot stand to look on a dead face living. It will make me mad. But he went on. There was a singing in his ears. Not me he came for, his mind crowed, harshly pounding like a heart in his head. Not me. It was her. No ghostly blade upon the throat, then. Only this, and this is so much worse.

As he reached the doors the cock crowed again and he cursed. The outer doors were a little open and a crisp morning chill crept in. Hugh ran a few steps, hurled the doors wide and stood peering fearfully out. The courtyard was empty, the sky above it violet. He ran across it and through the gate. Frost glowed in the darkness. He saw them hurrying for the forest and followed thoughtlessly. I must be sick, he thought, moving so slowly. Serafina! His mind called her. She should appear, summoned by thought, the helpful good beast of an old tale. But she slumbered on in her stall while her master foundered, wondering should he go back for her but not wishing to lose sight for a moment, even to blink, of his sister and the dark apparition that drew her swiftly on to where the trees waited.

How could they move so quickly? The Devil gave them wings. They were making for Ellwin Bridge, where the beck crossed the borders of good land and scrub, turning for its final drift into the forest. Here the trees came closest. Light grew, revealing outlines. A ridge of land hid them from his sight and he sobbed tearlessly for his damned snail's gait, sick inside, climbing a gentle rise as if it were a mountain. A stabbing pain was in his side. At the top he stood gasping. There they were. There. As he watched they merged into the side of the forest like woodlice into rotten bark.

He half ran, half fell down ragged banks and stumbled on, into the trees where darkness soon fell and branches barred his way sternly, flinging arrogant arms against his breast and demanding to know his business.

'Belle,' he tried to call, but a silly weak voice emerged. A bird laughed at him.

'Belle,' he said, standing still.

There was no sign to tell him the way. He fought through undergrowth, cutting with his knife, found an animal highway that ran into another, and another that crossed the first and turned away, deep into a trough like hell; on through rank, damp beds of slimy matter, on to scale slippery rocks whose cold summits showed him nothing, on and on till he burned with a cold hatred of the woods and the morning and John Heron, and fell upon his face in the mould.

He lay stretched for a while, then rose slowly, wet and weary, sitting upon a bank to wait for his racing nerves to still. The gossiping voice of the beck came to him. When he felt able, he rose warily and followed the sound till he reached its broad ferny banks. Looking up at the sky that showed high and smooth between the parted trees, he saw that the clouds had passed, and the tired glory of dawn had broken silently over the forest, closing the doors of the other world.

It was over and she'd gone forever.

Hugh sheathed his knife but started up and drew it again immediately when a bird flew low in front of him from a nearby tree. The blade stood stark before his eyes, the trace of blood set solid upon it and glistening darkly with an insect's sheen. The outlaw's knife. He thought he felt the handle twitch in his hand, but it was only the muscles in his palm. No. It would turn its pointed tip in the air, seek his heart, linger a moment to savour his terror then pierce him savagely to the core.

He saw his own blood spirt.

He awoke from a dream. No more blood! He shuddered, hurling the knife furiously into Ellwin Beck. It pocked the water and sank and the big circles soon faded. Wild-eyed, he stood gazing at the beck as if the knife might leap back at him, then tore the beautiful sheath with its delicate tooling from his body and threw that after. It floated away, catching briefly on the stones from time to time as it went, but freeing itself each time for its long journey. He did not watch it for long, but turned and followed the beck down to Ellwin Bridge and walked from there to the house without a backward look.

When he came into the courtyard it was full light. Some servants were abroad, shamefaced and haggard. They looked sulkily and boldly at him, he thought, raising his head and drawing a deep breath, striding into the house and up the stairs to Harlock's apartment. Harlock was awake, sitting up in bed in a nightshirt with his head in his hands.

'Confound it, Rennock,' he groaned, 'the damn thing pains me more since it was pulled.'

'Your son gives orders in your stead,' Hugh said brusquely. 'I'm ordered away.'

Harlock looked about the room with old, fearful eyes. 'They said I did wrong,' he said. 'I told them. It was not my fault.'

'Who said?'

'She. And him! Master Storksleg. Where's Sim?' He lay back with fluttering lids coming down on upturning eyes, like a dying man, lowering his wide head onto the pillow as if it were priceless glass, then drew in a long breath through gritted teeth lined with dark dried blood. 'I did no wrong,' he said, 'I did not, I did not, I did not. I could send them all begging.'

'The knife you gave me was cursed,' Hugh said sullenly. 'I've lost my sister.'

Harlock's eyes popped open, wide and yellowish. 'Where is it?' he asked.

'What?'

'Your knife,' Harlock said impatiently, 'your knife, your knife,' just as he had before taking the head.

He is mad, thought Hugh. 'I've lost it,' he said.

'That knife,' said Harlock distantly, 'that knife was the finest I ever saw. Where do you suppose the villain got it? Who did he kill for it? Lost?'

'Lost,' said Hugh. 'Gone. Gone.'

The eyes once more closed. 'You can have another,' said Harlock. 'There are plenty. And the sheath?'

'Lost.'

Harlock sat up and a smell of stale wine came with him. 'Why so mopish?' he said and brought his feet to the floor. His legs were inappropriately thin about the ankles, white as lilies. 'Come. We'll go to the armoury, and you may choose,' he said, and walked across the room and turned, smiling at Hugh. His eyes were horrible, black-rimmed and blooded where some threads had burst and flooded the whites.

Night had gone and light was come, and all the worst things were true. Hugh walked out and went down through the house, out into the yard, where he called for his horse. It was very cold as he waited, watching small birds hop on the stones. Winter would be hard.

A sleepy groom appeared, leading Serafina.

'Have my things sent on,' said Hugh, preparing to mount but pausing as a qualm of sickness passed through him. He leaned his cold, sweating brow upon the mare's warm flank and her gentle grey head turned towards him.

'Do not leave me,' he said to her soft eyes. 'Do not leave me.'

elle had left the cage open.

The small green parrot stood on her broad window sill, shifting from one foot to the other steadfastly, looking down mild-eyed. He'd flown before, many times inside, but never had he looked at such pure round emptiness as this cold world calling at his gnarled yellow feet. He was unhurried, considering.

He stood still, darting his thick beak in amongst his breast feathers, once, twice. His round eye blinked. Then he launched himself in heavy flight downwards, landing in a bush that quivered at his arrival, and after a while from there to a tree and then to another, and so on for a while, alighting here and there till he reached the forest. And there he climbed a little higher and a little higher, till he was confronted at last by the fulness of the shimmering white sky shaking itself out like an apron over the treetops, and a hawk came in low and took him in a second.